BENNY AND PENNY

IN

THE TOY BREAKER

Where is he?
I don't see him.

A TOON BOOK BY

GEOFFREY HAYES

TOON BOOKS IS AN IMPRINT OF CANDLEWICK PRESS

A JUNIOR LIBRARY GUILD SELECTION

BANK STREET COLLEGE OF EDUCATION
Best Children's Books of the Year

KIRKUS BEST OF '09 CONTINUING SERIES

For Leigh Stein,
who is Penny in disguise

Editorial Director: FRANÇOISE MOULY

Book Design: FRANÇOISE MOULY & JONATHAN BENNETT

GEOFFREY HAYES' artwork was drawn in colored pencil.

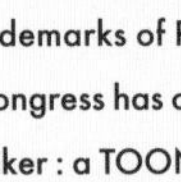

A TOON Book™ © 2010 RAW Junior, LLC, 27 Greene Street, New York, NY 10013. TOON Books® is an imprint of Candlewick Press, 99 Dover Street, Somerville, MA 02144. No part of this book may be used or reproduced in any manner whatsoever without written permission except in the case of brief quotations embodied in critical articles and reviews. TOON Books®, LITTLE LIT® and TOON Into Reading!™ are trademarks of RAW Junior, LLC. All rights reserved. Printed in Dongguan, Guangdong, China by Toppan Leefung. The Library of Congress has cataloged the hardcover edition as follows:

Hayes, Geoffrey.   Benny and Penny in the toy breaker : a TOON Book / by Geoffrey Hayes.

    p. cm.   Summary: When their cousin Bo comes to visit, Benny and Penny hide their toys and try to go on a treasure hunt without him, but Bo will not stop pestering them.   ISBN: 978-1-935179-07-8 (hardcover)

  1. Graphic novels. [1. Graphic novels. 2. Bullies–Fiction. 3. Brothers and sisters–Fiction. 4. Cousins–Fiction. 5. Mice–Fiction.] I. Title.

II. Title: Toy breaker.   PZ7.7.H39Bdm 2010   [E]–dc22   2009038066

                ISBN: 978-1-935179-28-3 (paperback)

            13 14 15 16 17 18 TPN 10 9 8 7 6 5 4 3 2 1

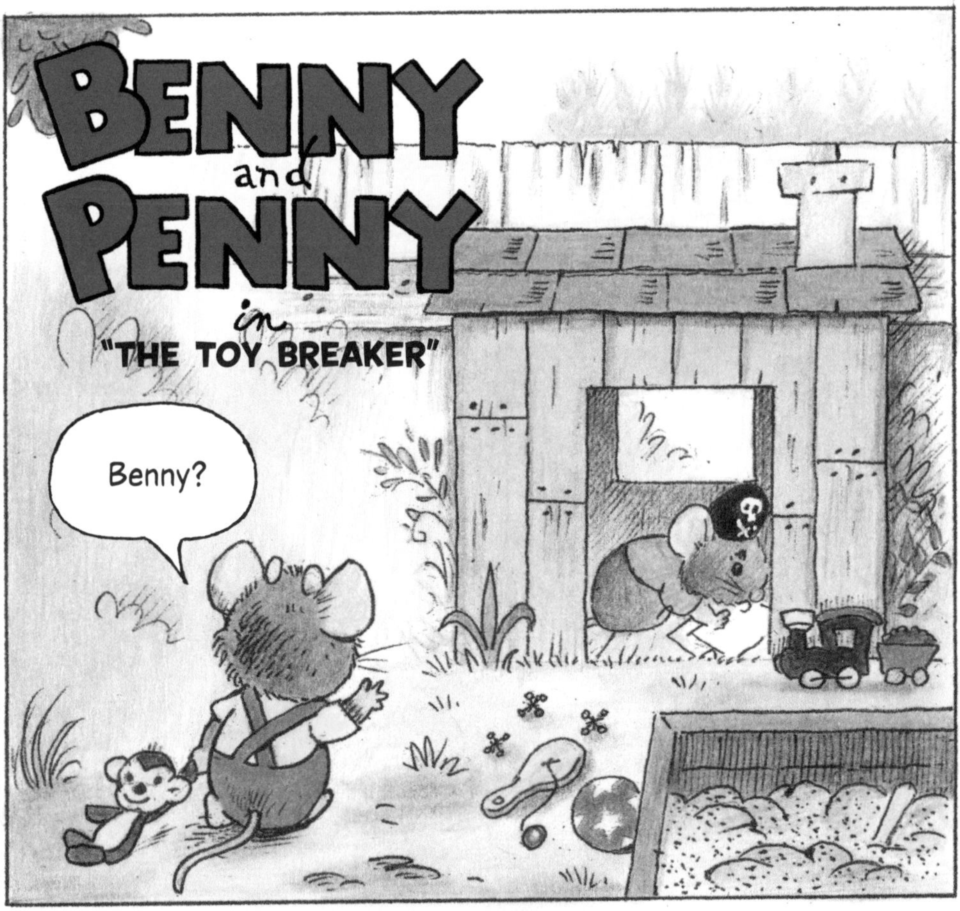
BENNY and PENNY
in
"THE TOY BREAKER"
Benny?

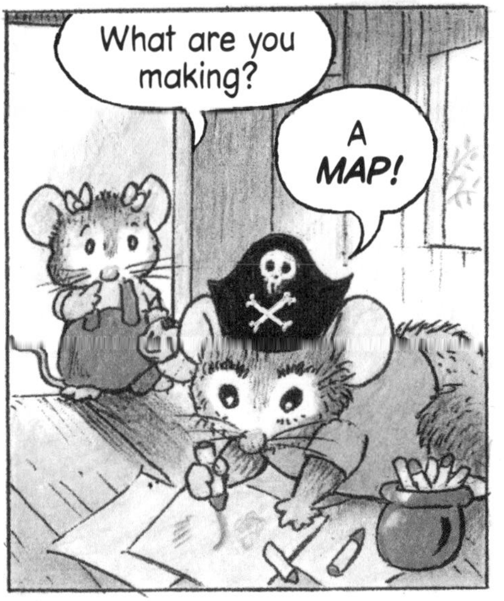
What are you making?
A MAP!

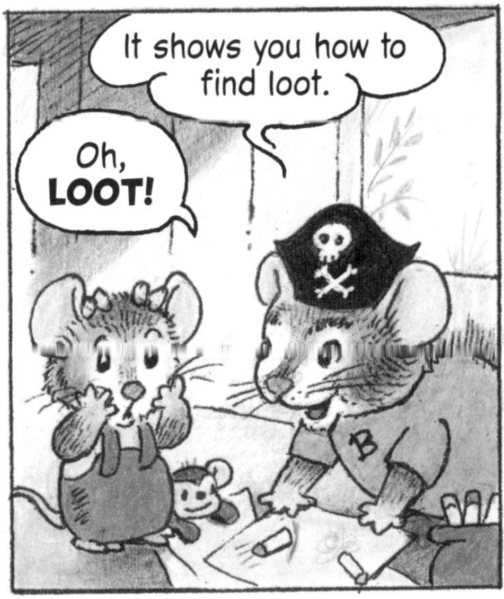
It shows you how to find loot.
Oh, LOOT!

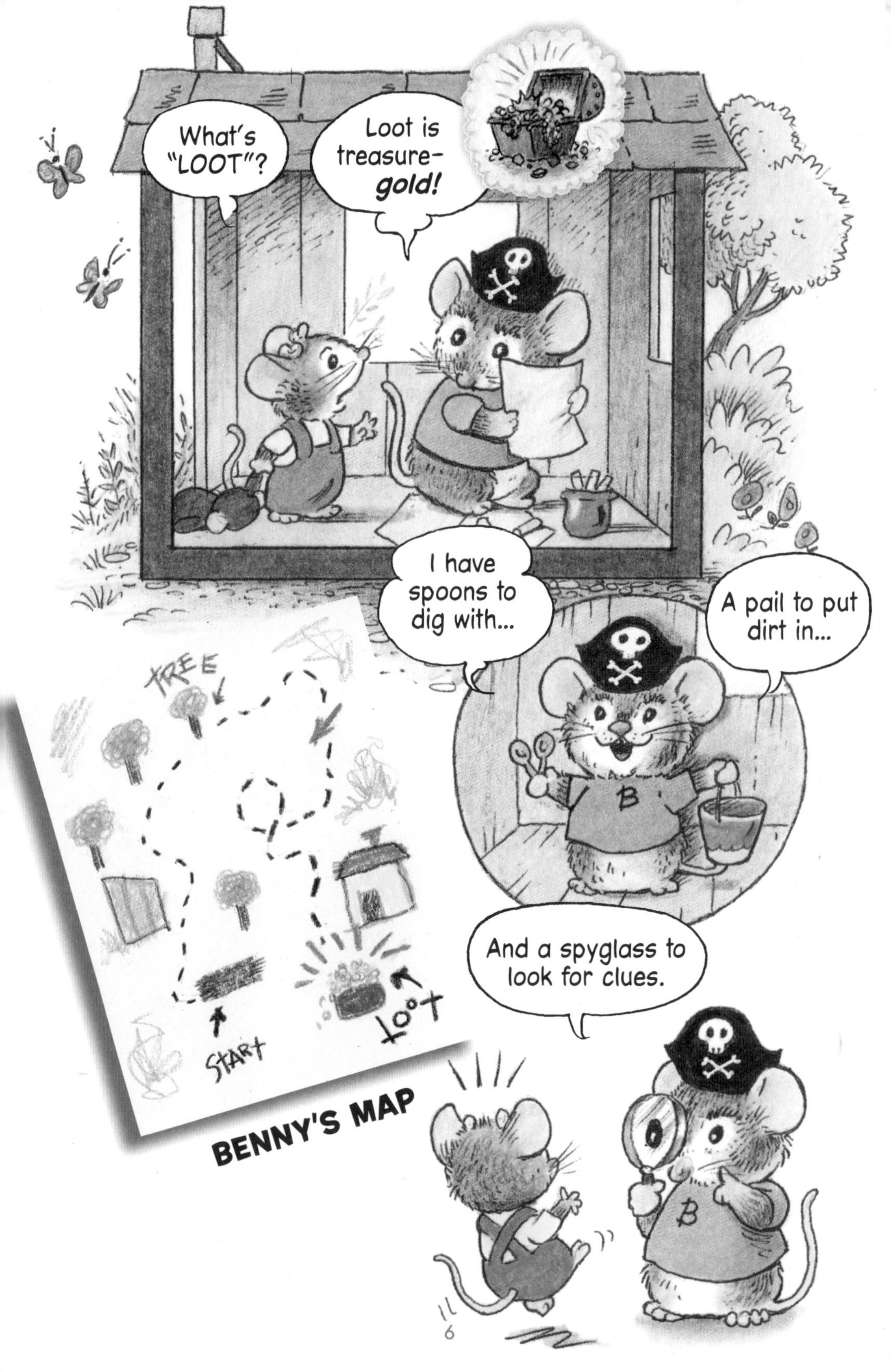

What's "LOOT"?
Loot is treasure-*gold!*
I have spoons to dig with...
A pail to put dirt in...
And a spyglass to look for clues.
TREE
START
LOOT
BENNY'S MAP

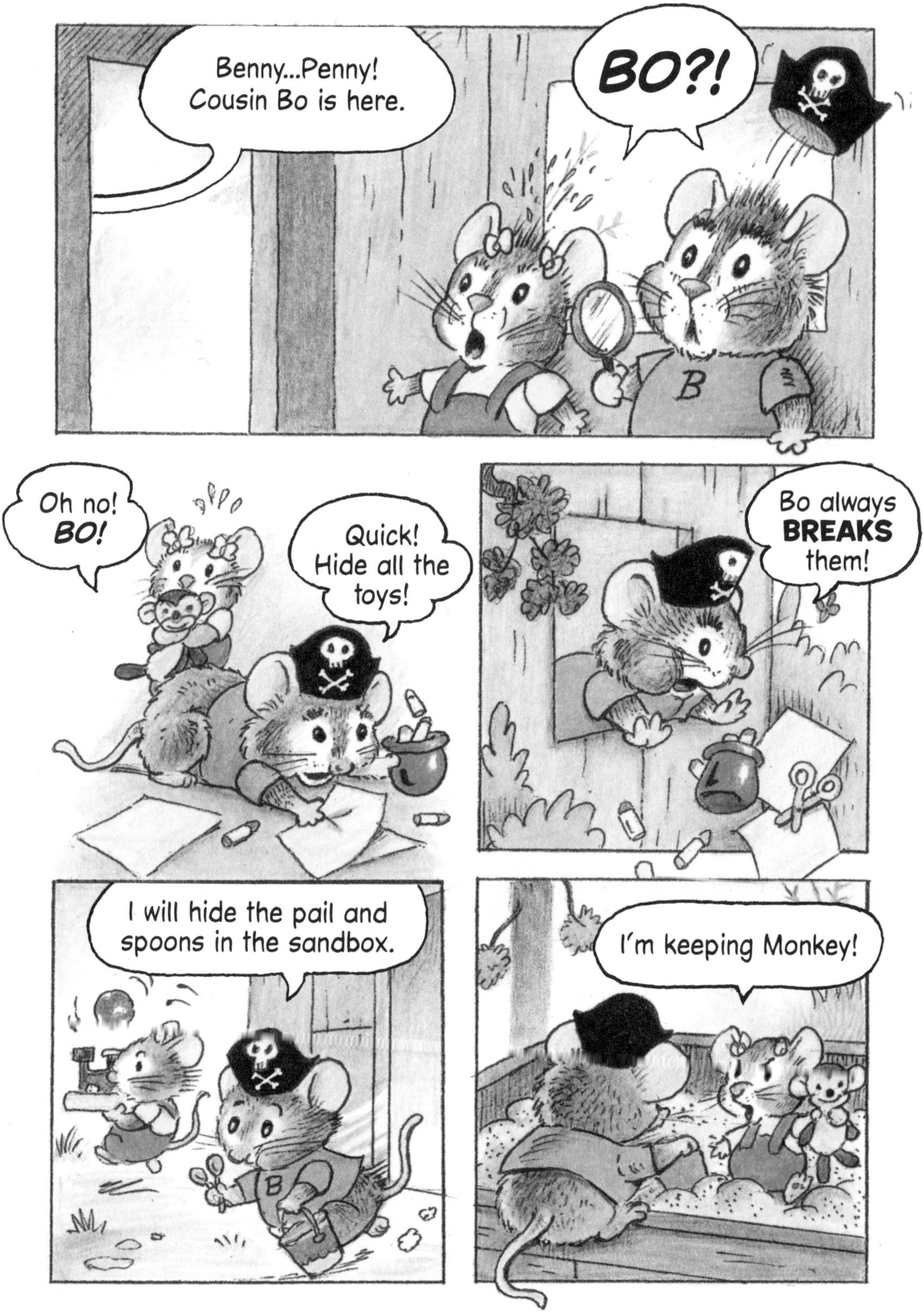
Benny...Penny! Cousin Bo is here.
BO?!
Oh no! BO!
Quick! Hide all the toys!
Bo always BREAKS them!
I will hide the pail and spoons in the sandbox.
I'm keeping Monkey!

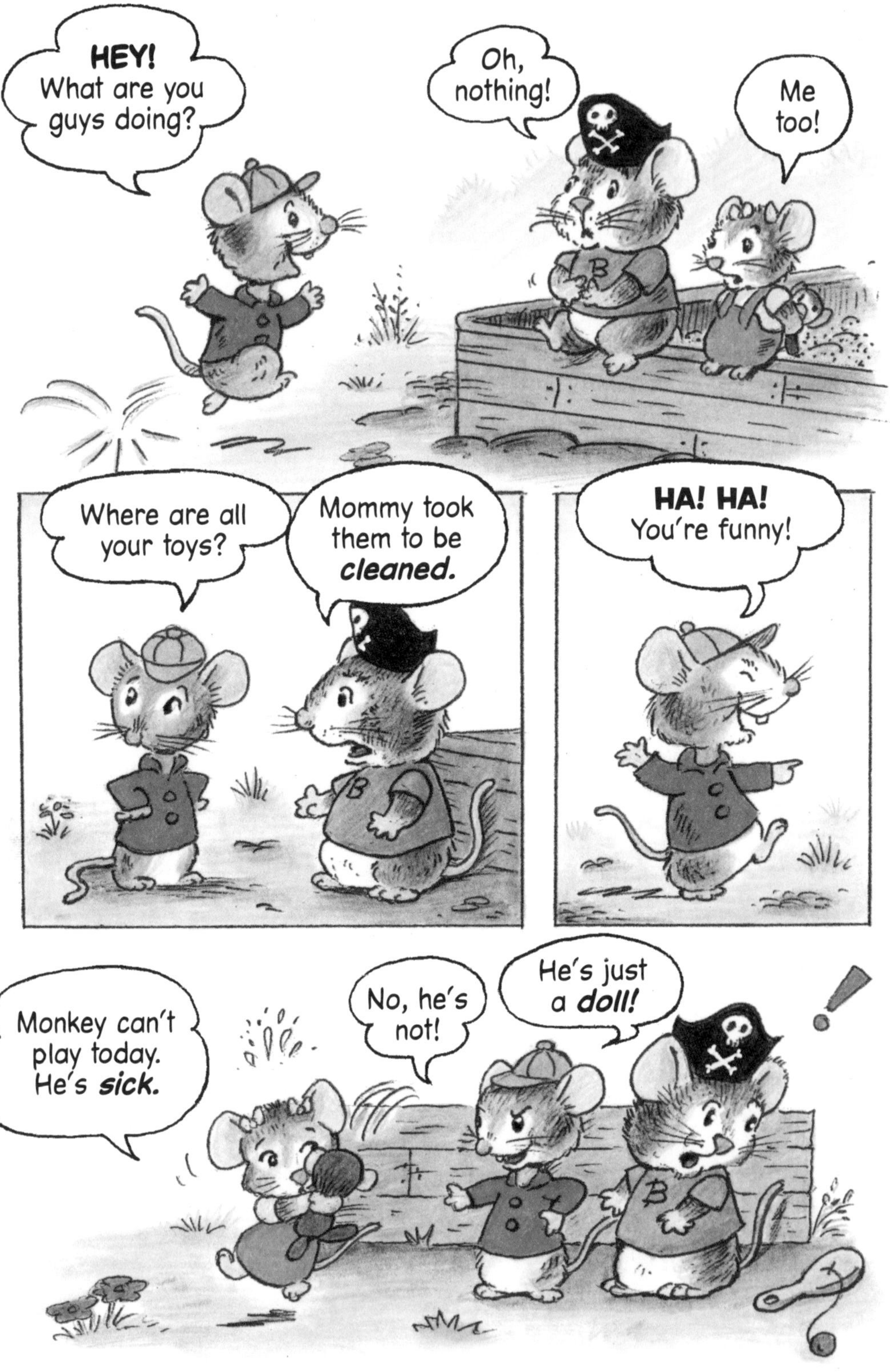
HEY! What are you guys doing?
Oh, nothing!
Me too!
Where are all your toys?
Mommy took them to be cleaned.
HA! HA! You're funny!
Monkey can't play today. He's sick.
No, he's not!
He's just a doll!

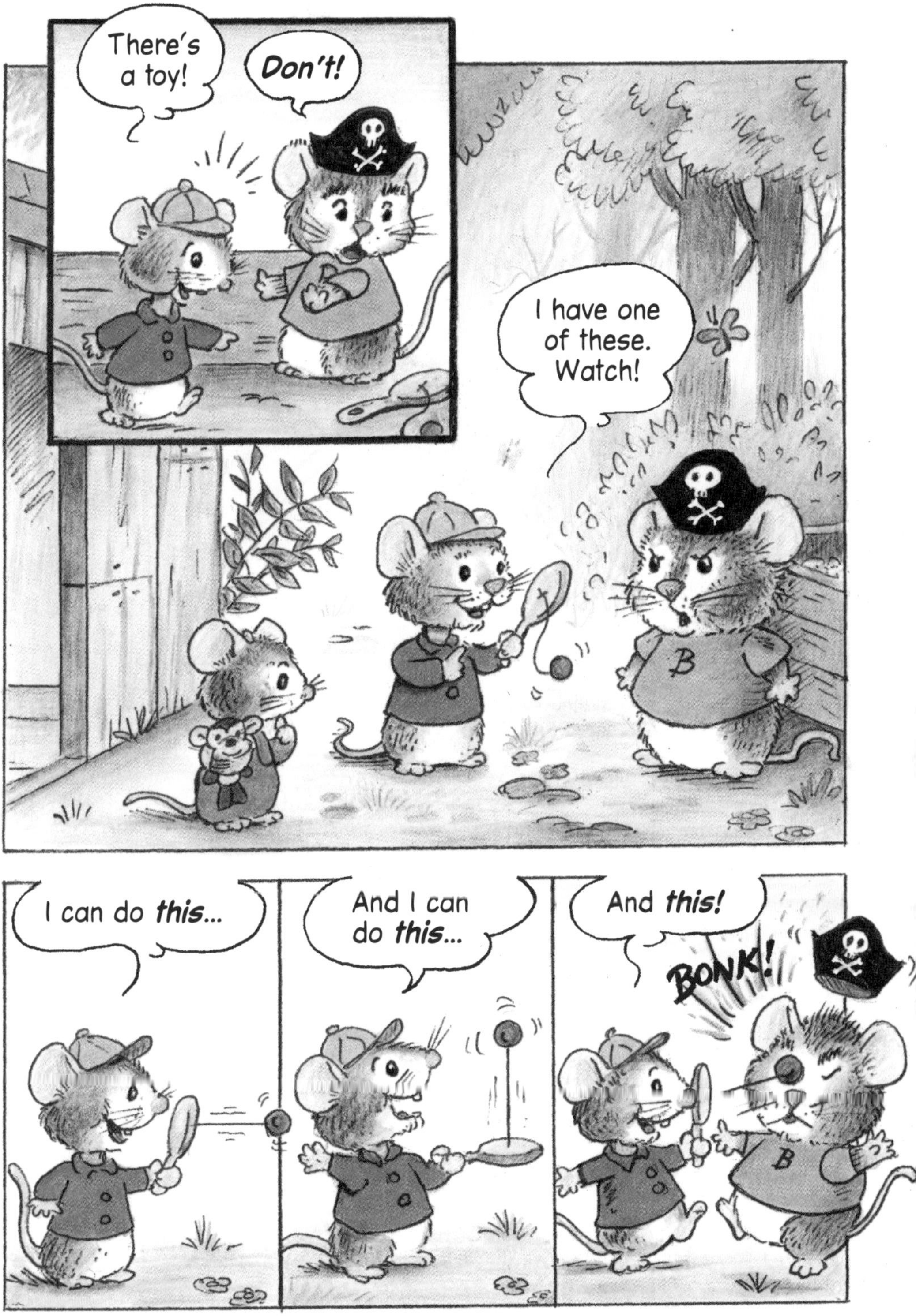
There's a toy!
Don't!
I have one of these. Watch!
I can do this...
And I can do this...
And this!
BONK!

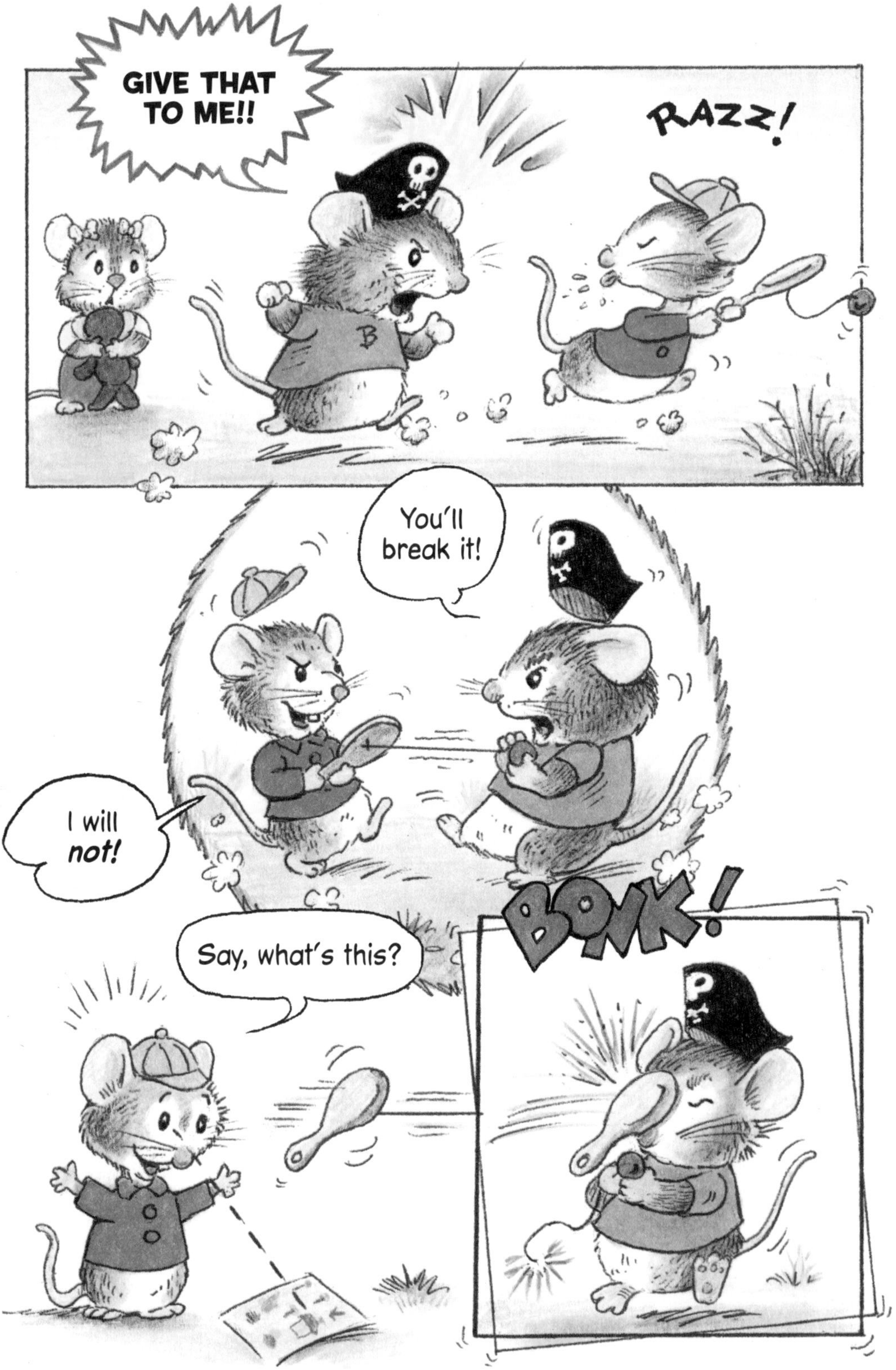
GIVE THAT TO ME!!
RAZZ!
You'll break it!
I will *not!*
Say, what's this?
BONK!

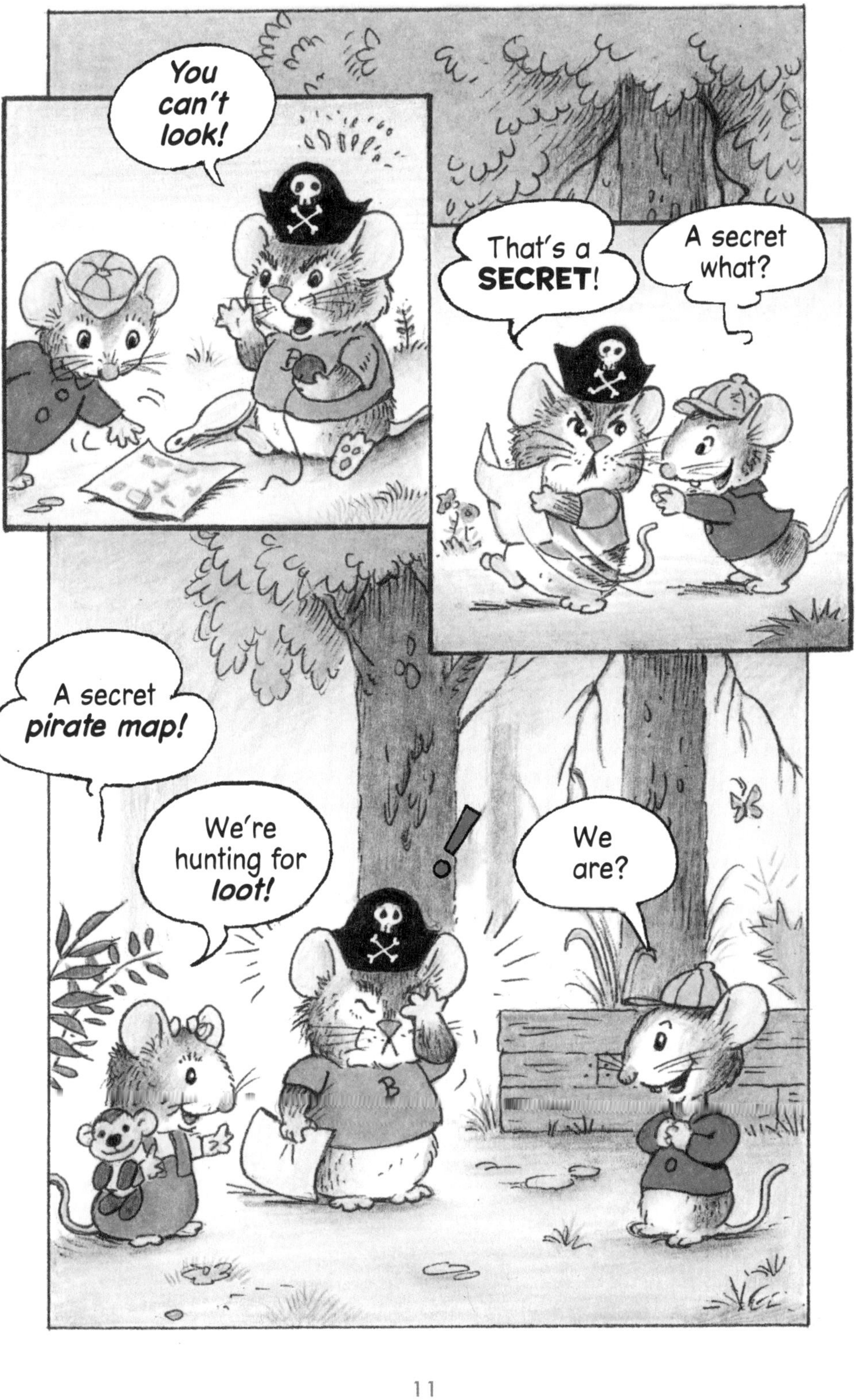
You can't look!
That's a SECRET!
A secret what?
A secret pirate map!
We're hunting for loot!
!
We are?

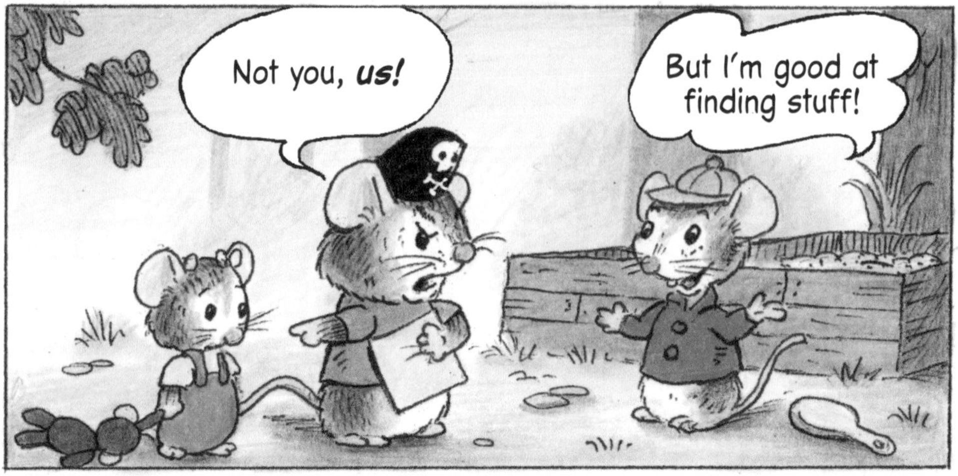
Not you, ***us!***
But I'm good at finding stuff!

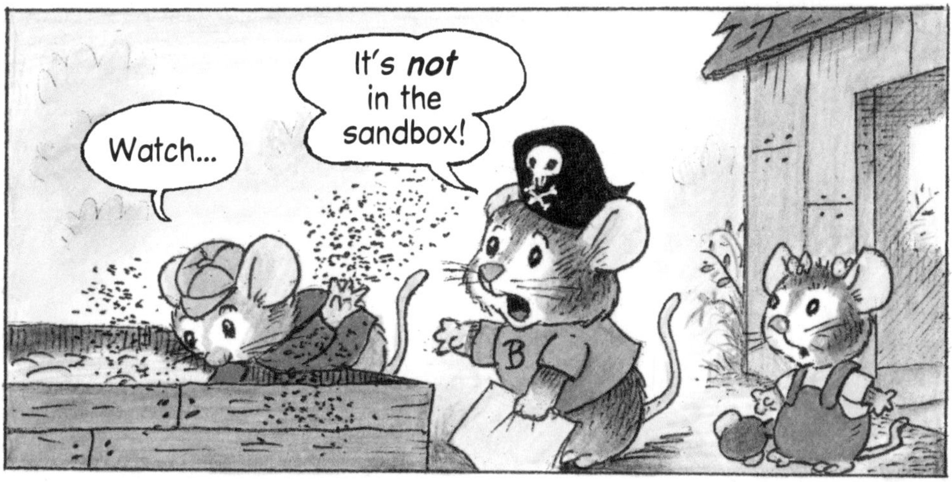
Watch...
It's ***not*** in the sandbox!

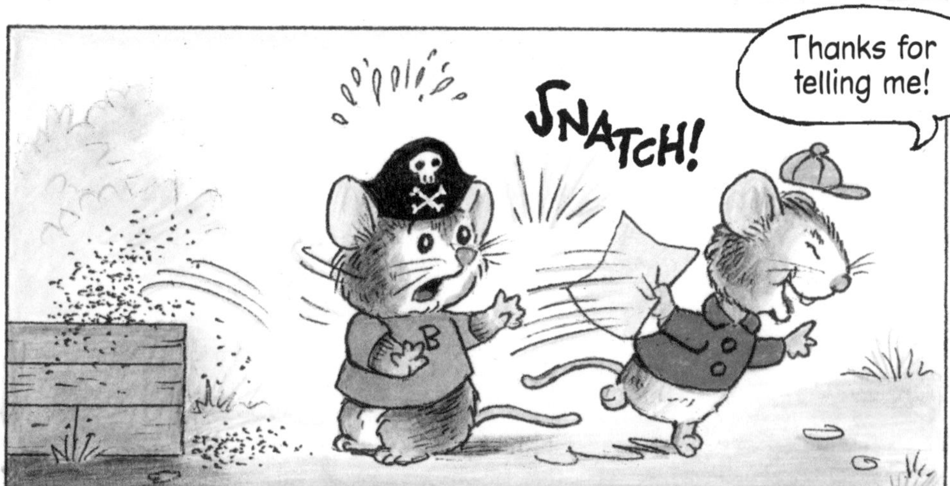
SNATCH!
Thanks for telling me!

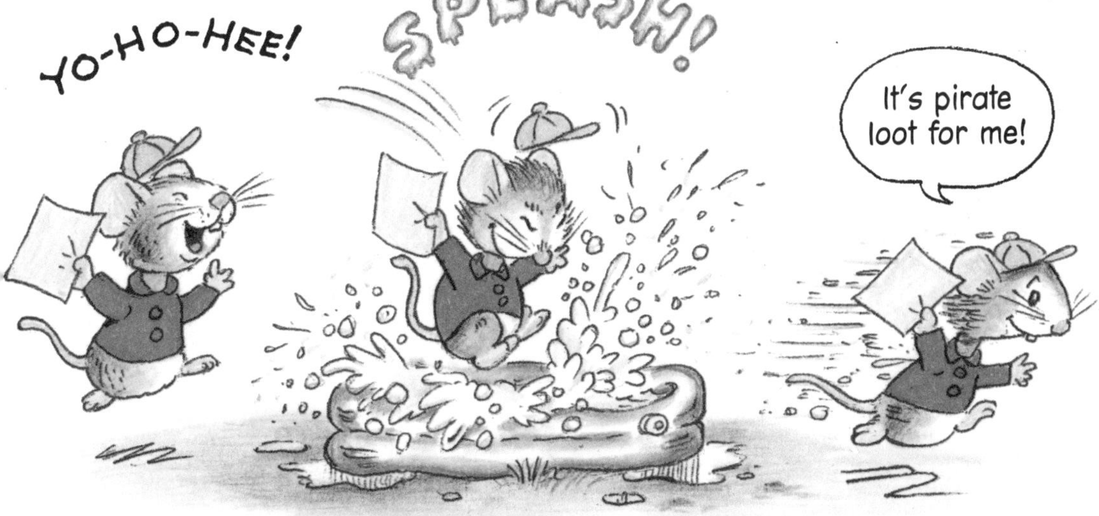
YO-HO-HEE!
SPLASH!
It's pirate loot for me!

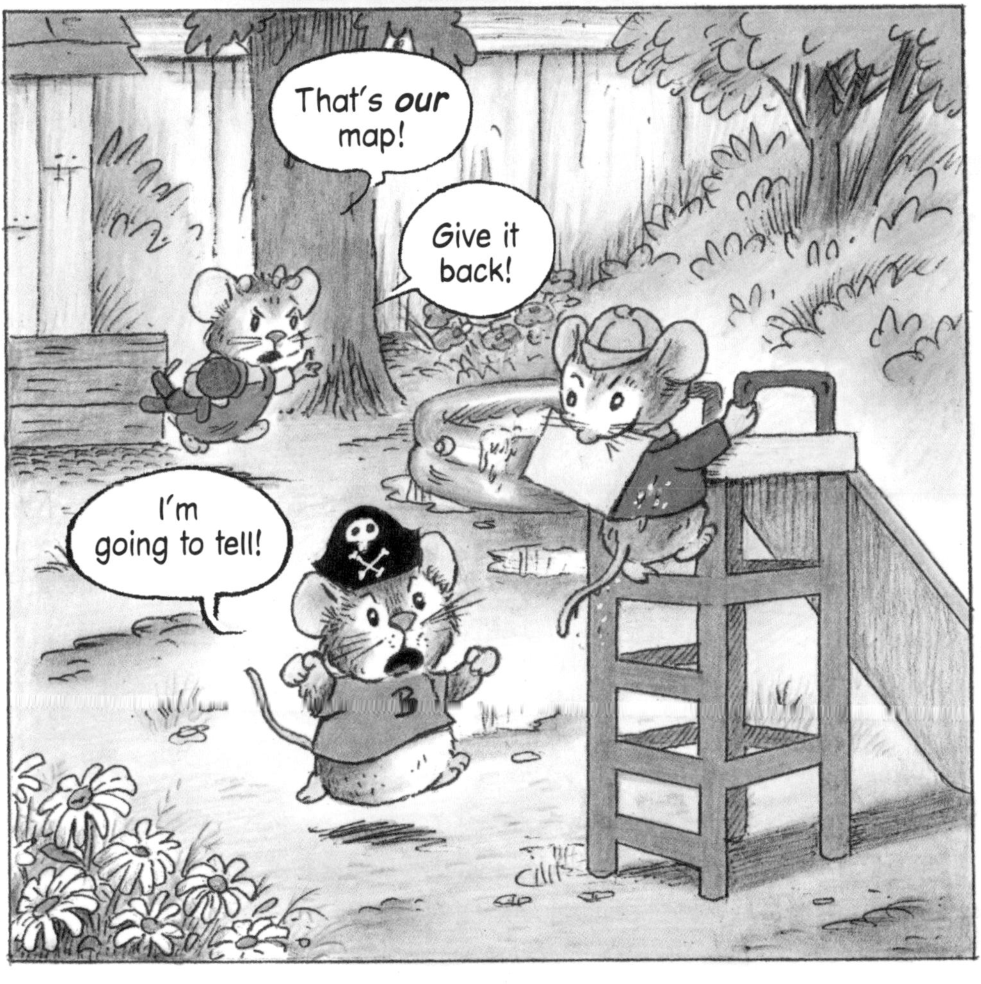
That's *our* map!
Give it back!
I'm going to tell!

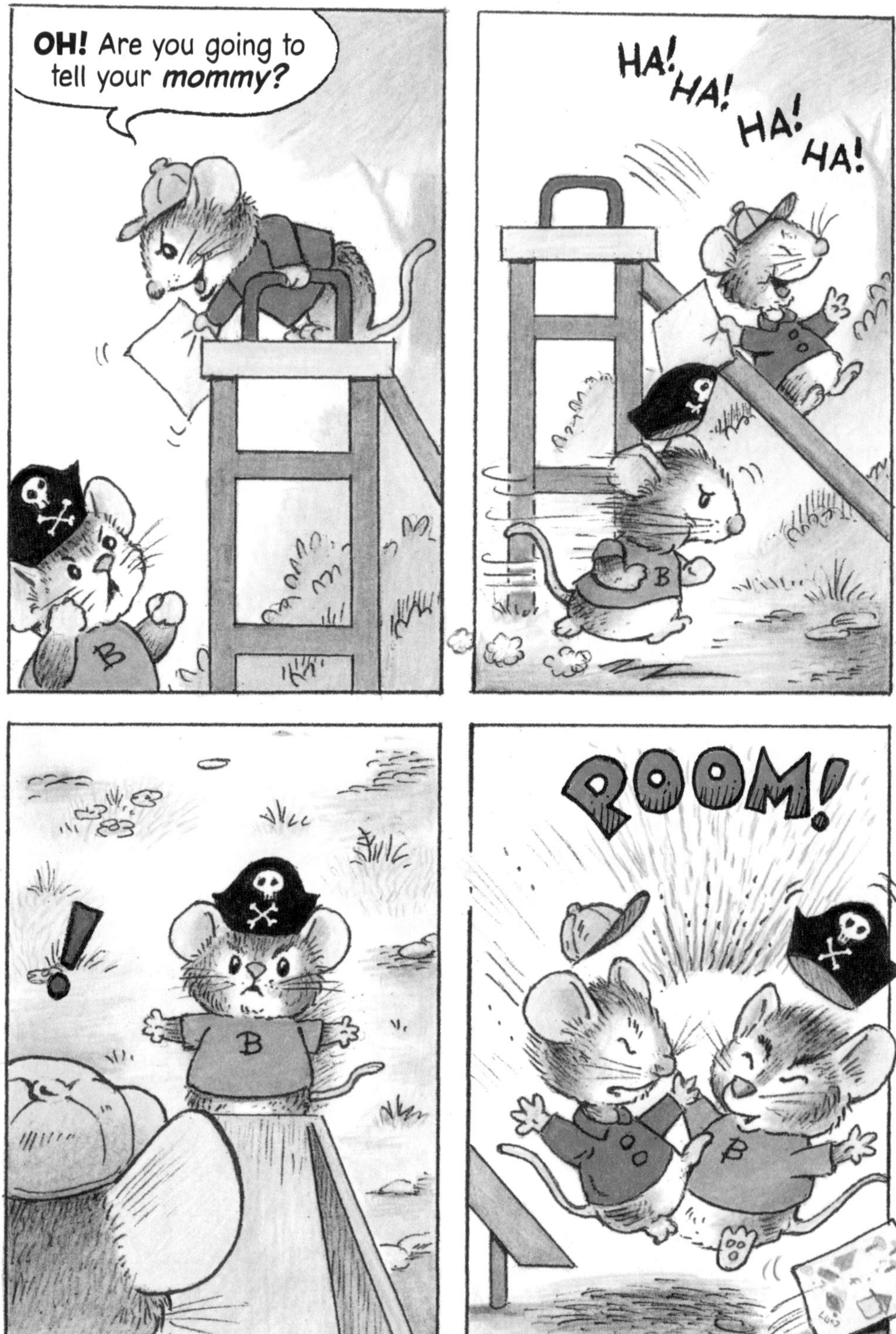
OH! Are you going to tell your mommy?
HA! HA! HA! HA!
POOM!

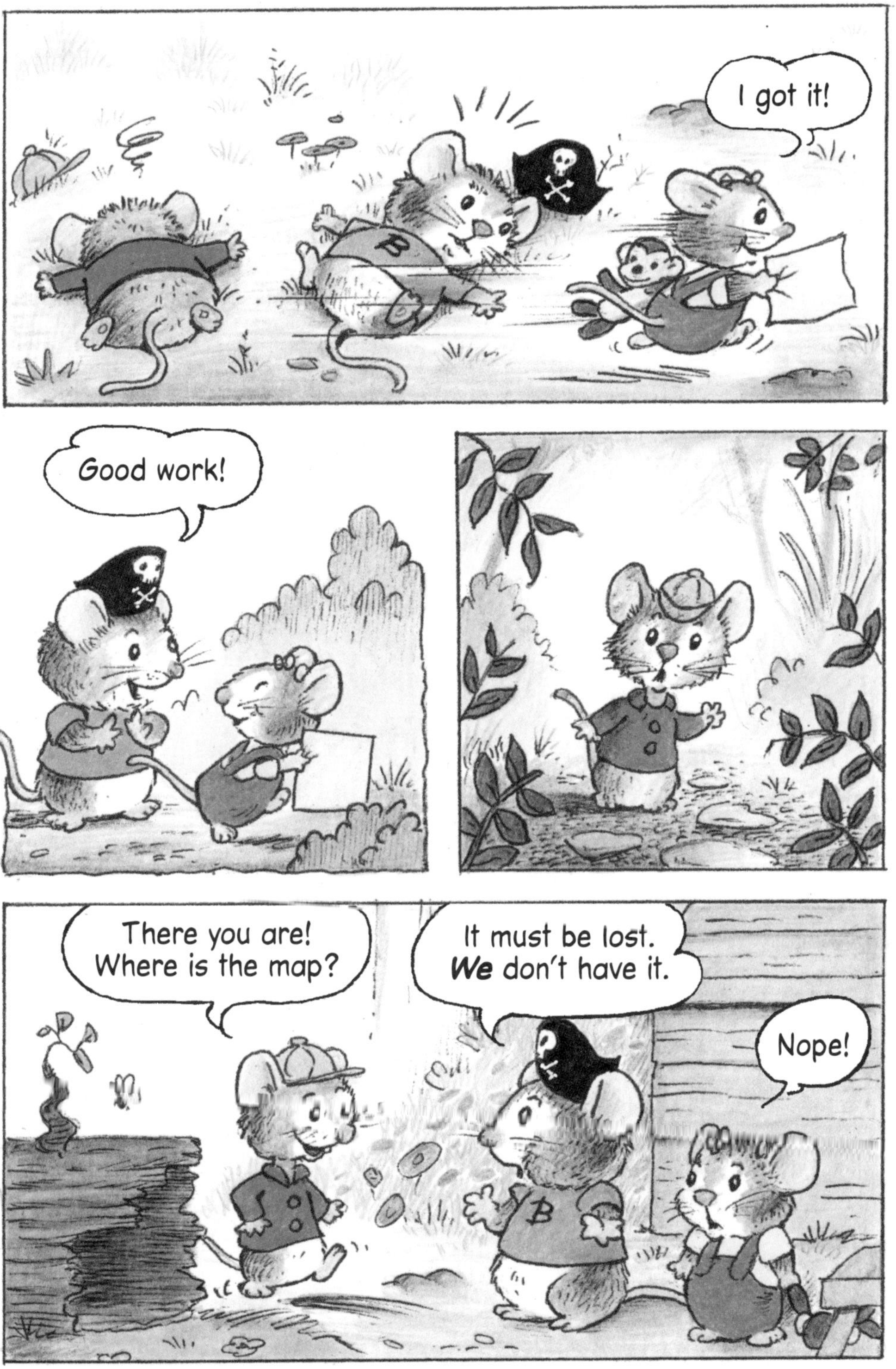
I got it!
Good work!
There you are! Where is the map?
It must be lost. **We** don't have it.
Nope!

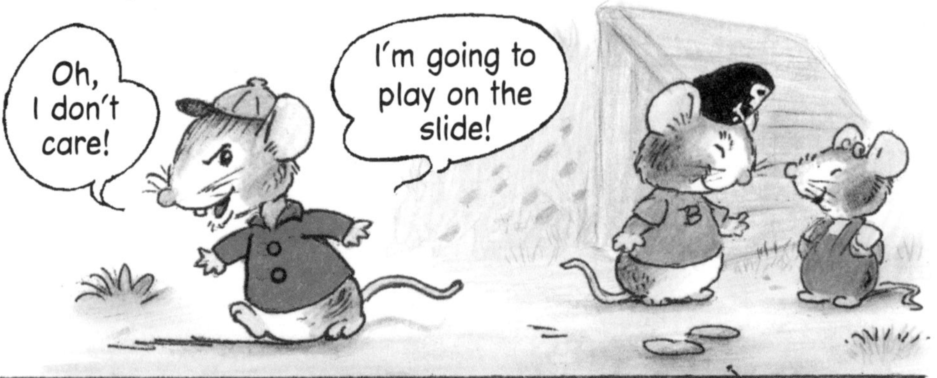
Oh,
I don't
care!
I'm going to
play on the
slide!
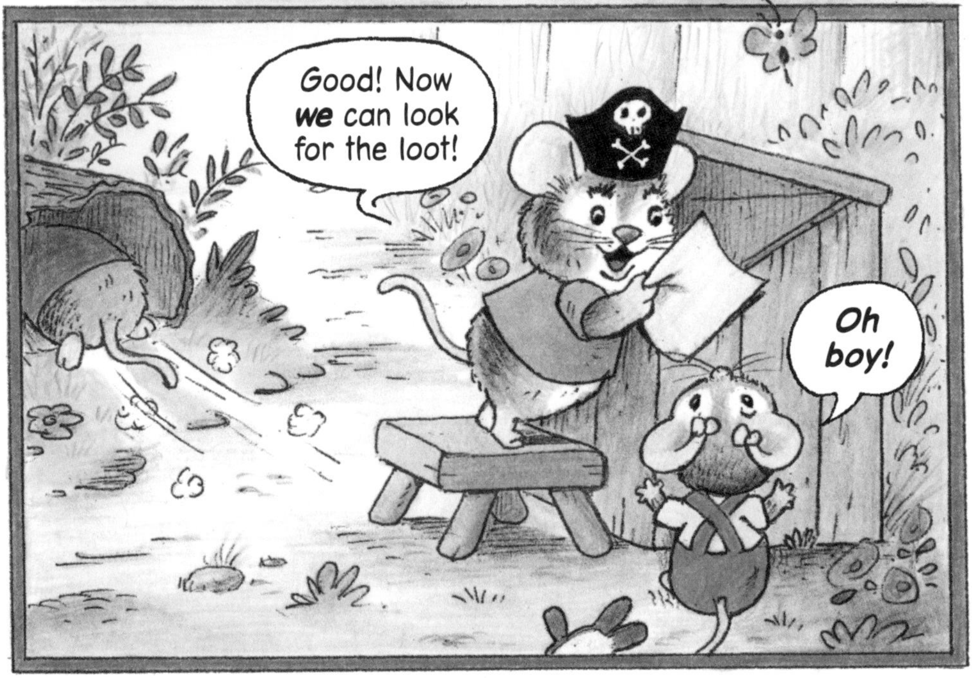
Good! Now
we can look
for the loot!
**Oh
boy!**
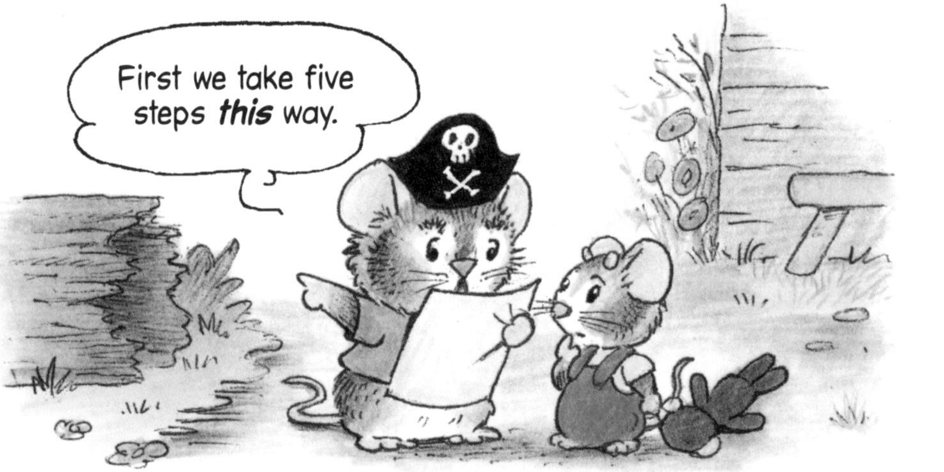
First we take five
steps **this** way.

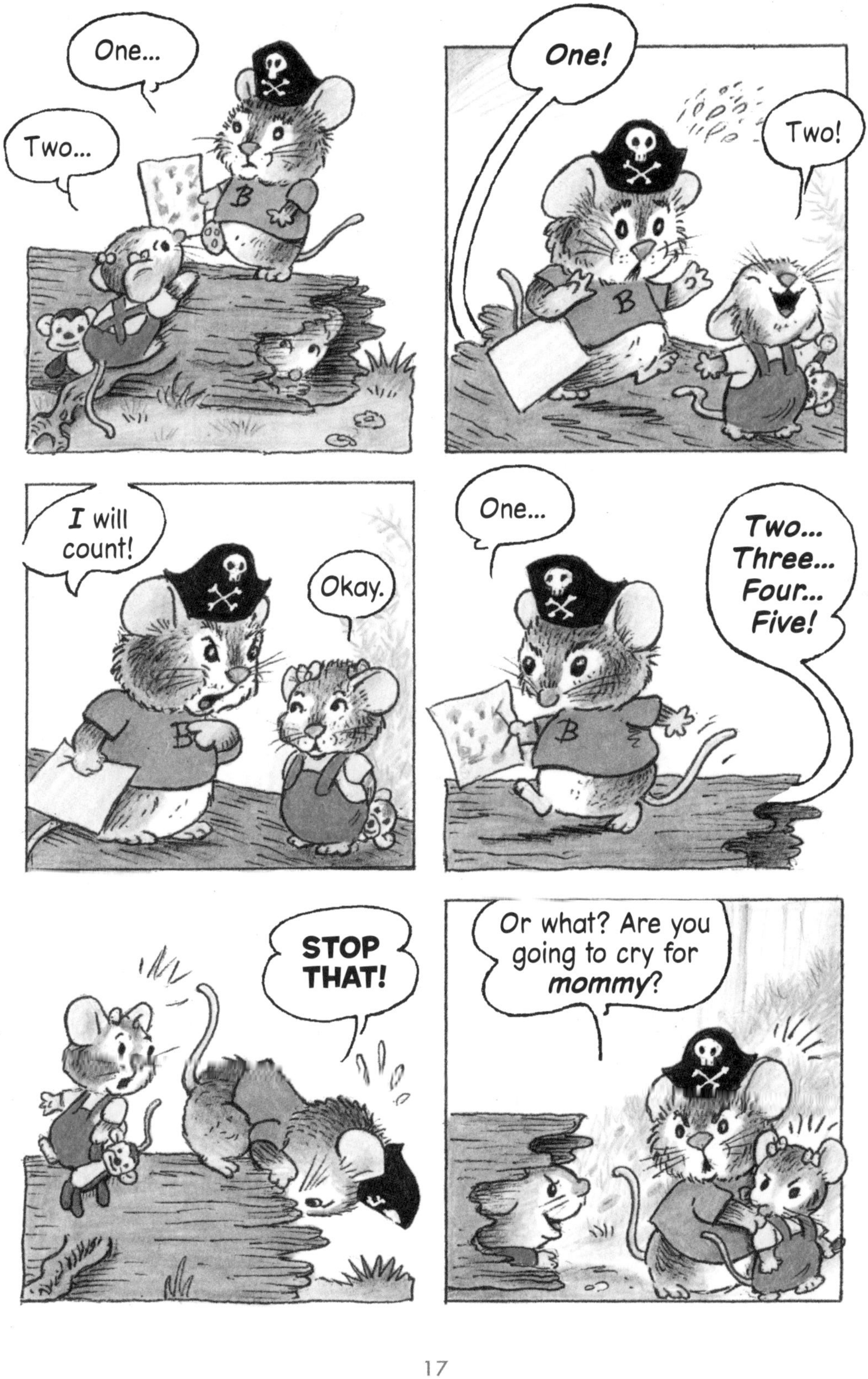
One...
Two...
One!
Two!
I will count!
Okay.
One...
Two... Three... Four... Five!
STOP THAT!
Or what? Are you going to cry for mommy?

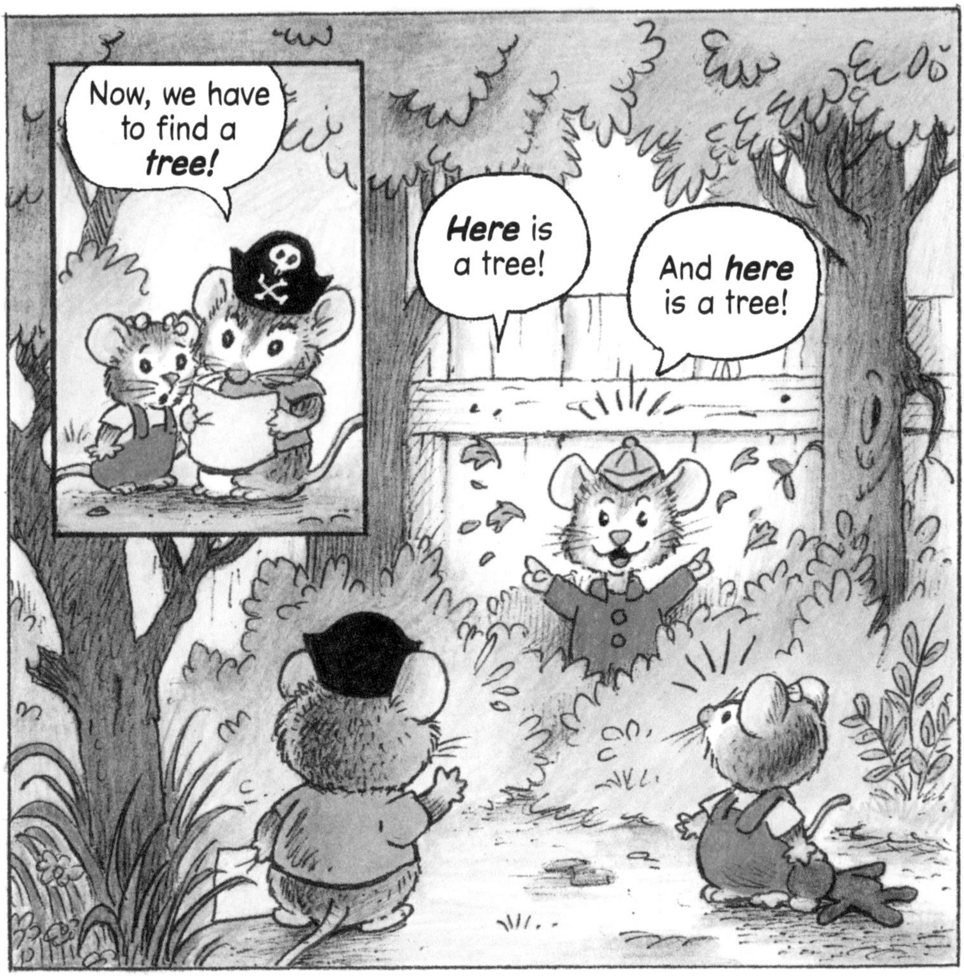
Now, we have to find a ***tree!***
Here is a tree!
And ***here*** is a tree!

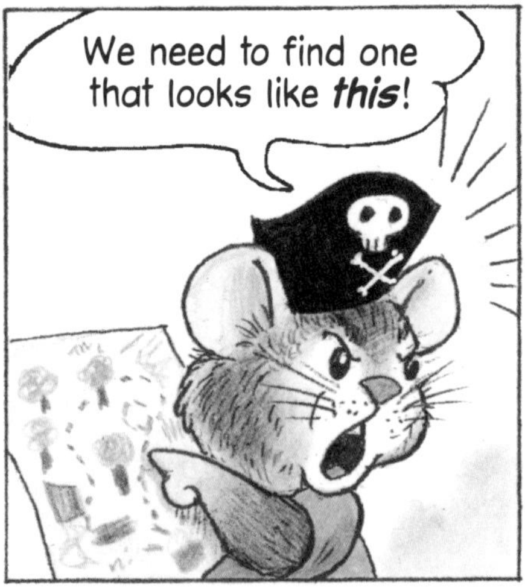
We need to find one that looks like ***this***!

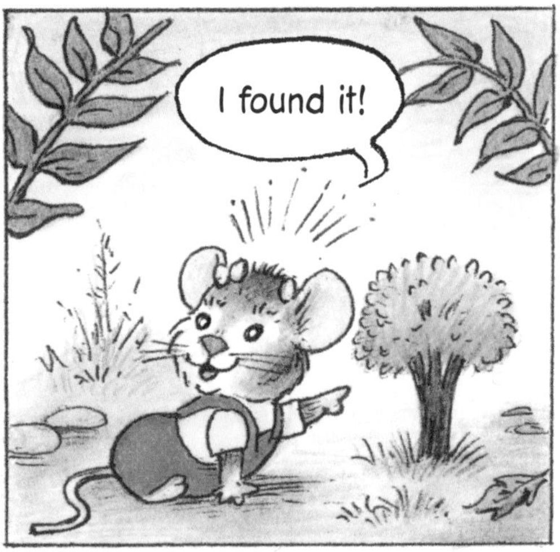
I found it!

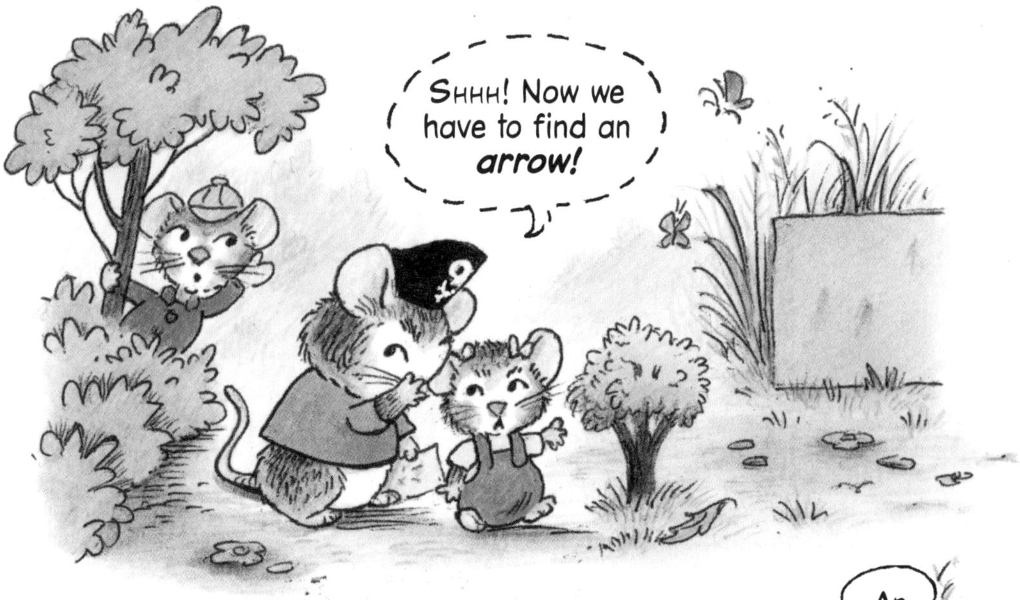
SHHH! Now we have to find an *arrow!*

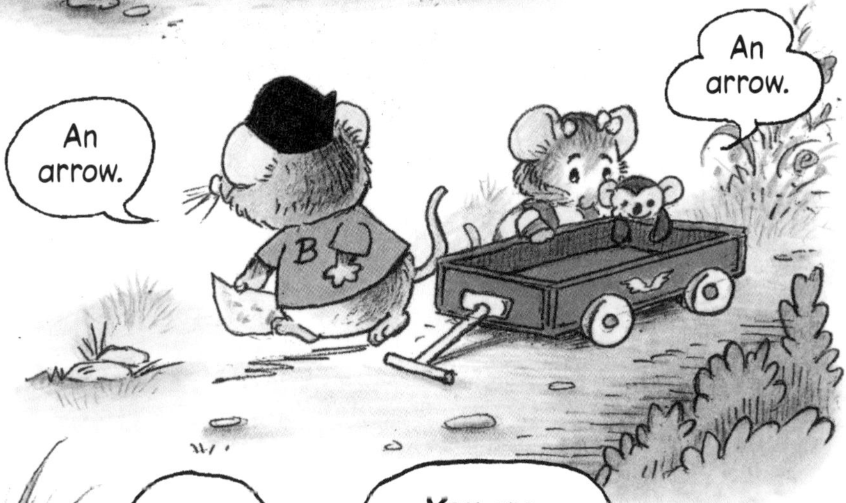
An arrow.
An arrow.

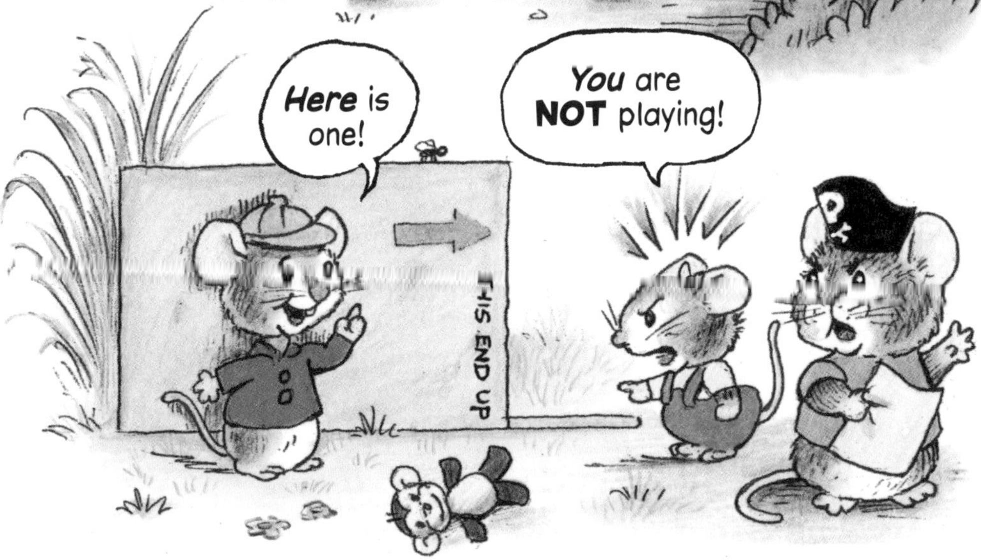
Here is one!
THIS END UP
You are **NOT** playing!

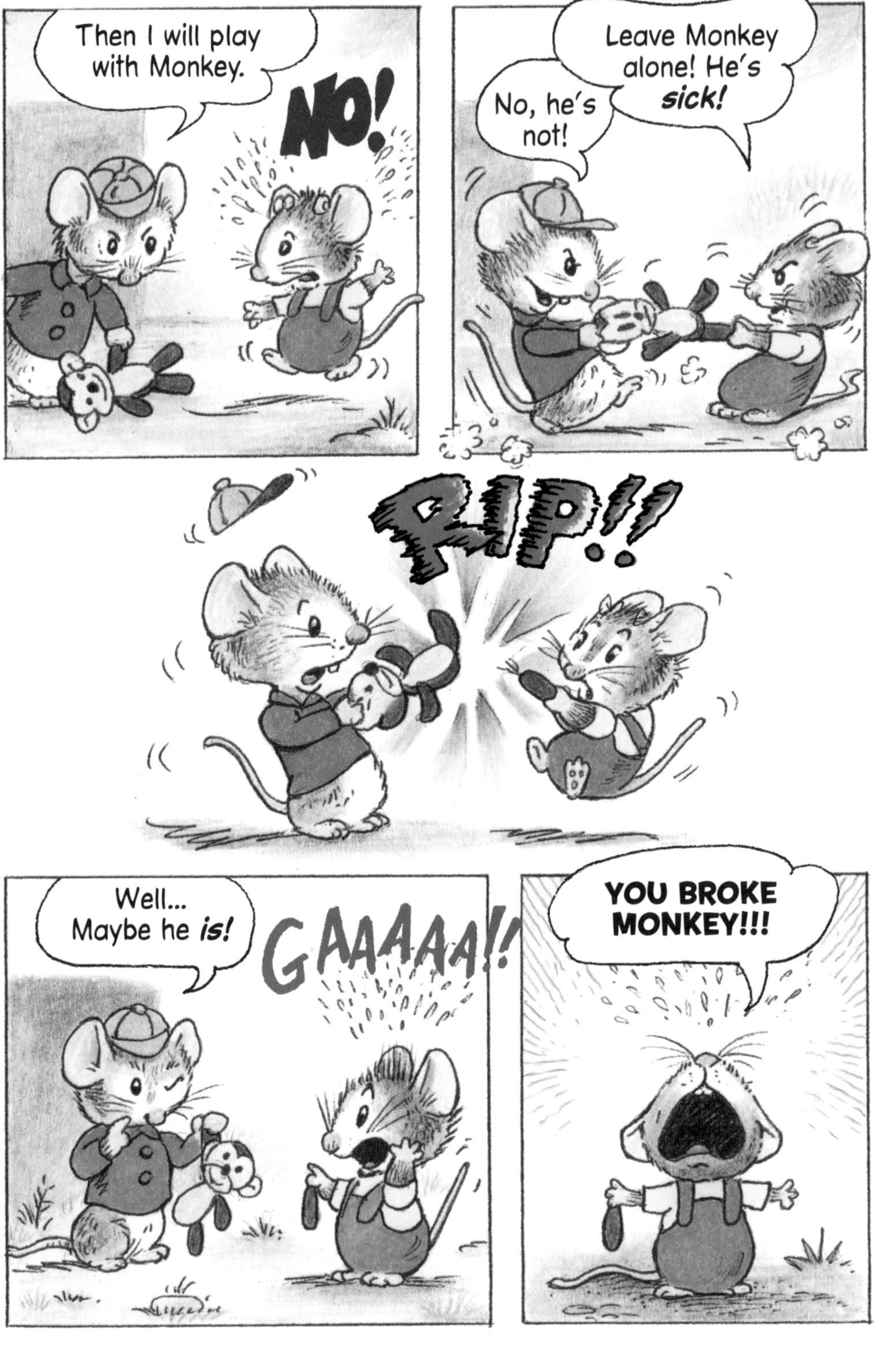
Then I will play with Monkey.
NO!
Leave Monkey alone! He's *sick!*
No, he's not!
RIP!!
Well... Maybe he *is!*
GAAAAA!!
YOU BROKE MONKEY!!!

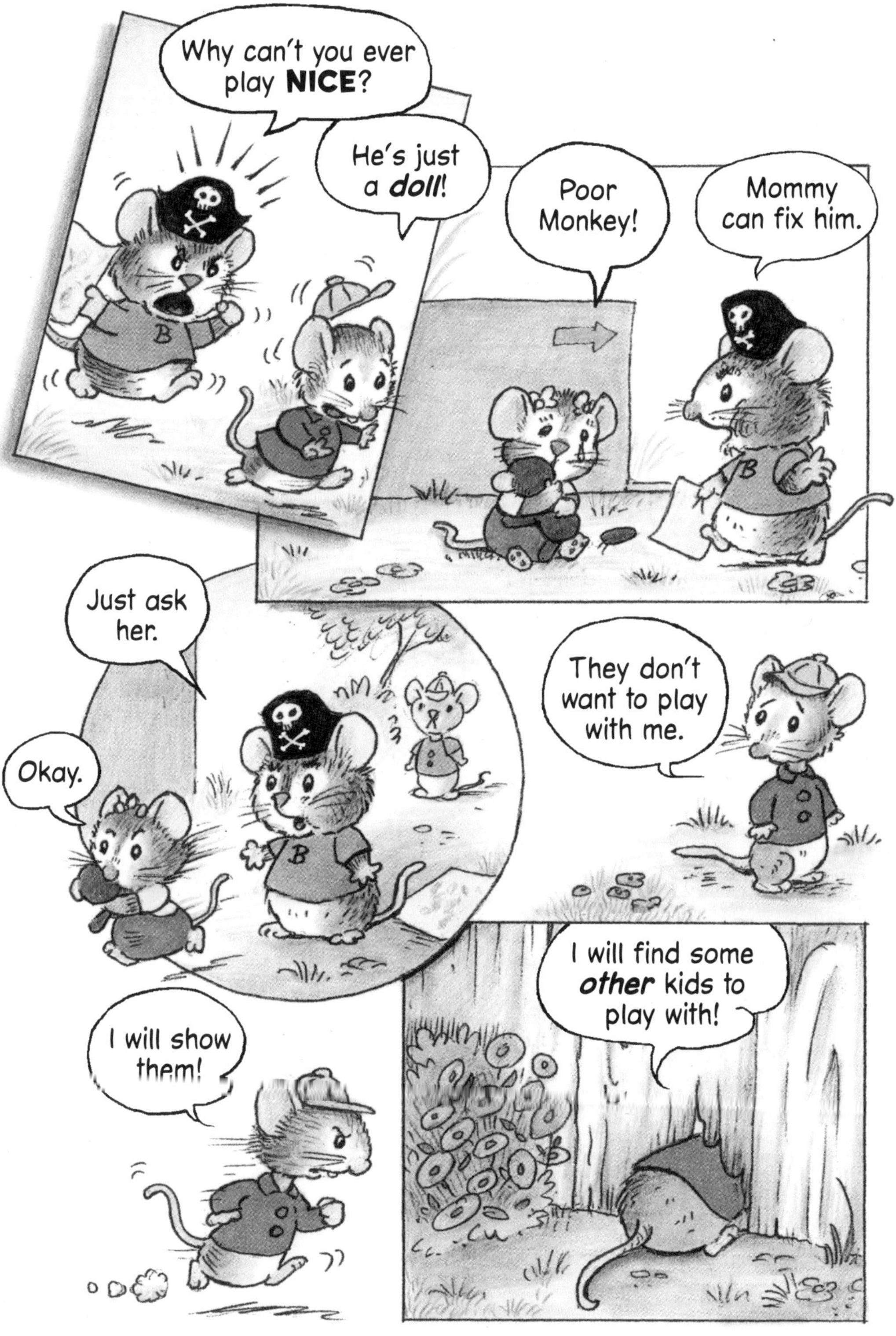
Why can't you ever play **NICE**?
He's just a ***doll***!
Poor Monkey!
Mommy can fix him.
Just ask her.
Okay.
They don't want to play with me.
I will show them!
I will find some ***other*** kids to play with!

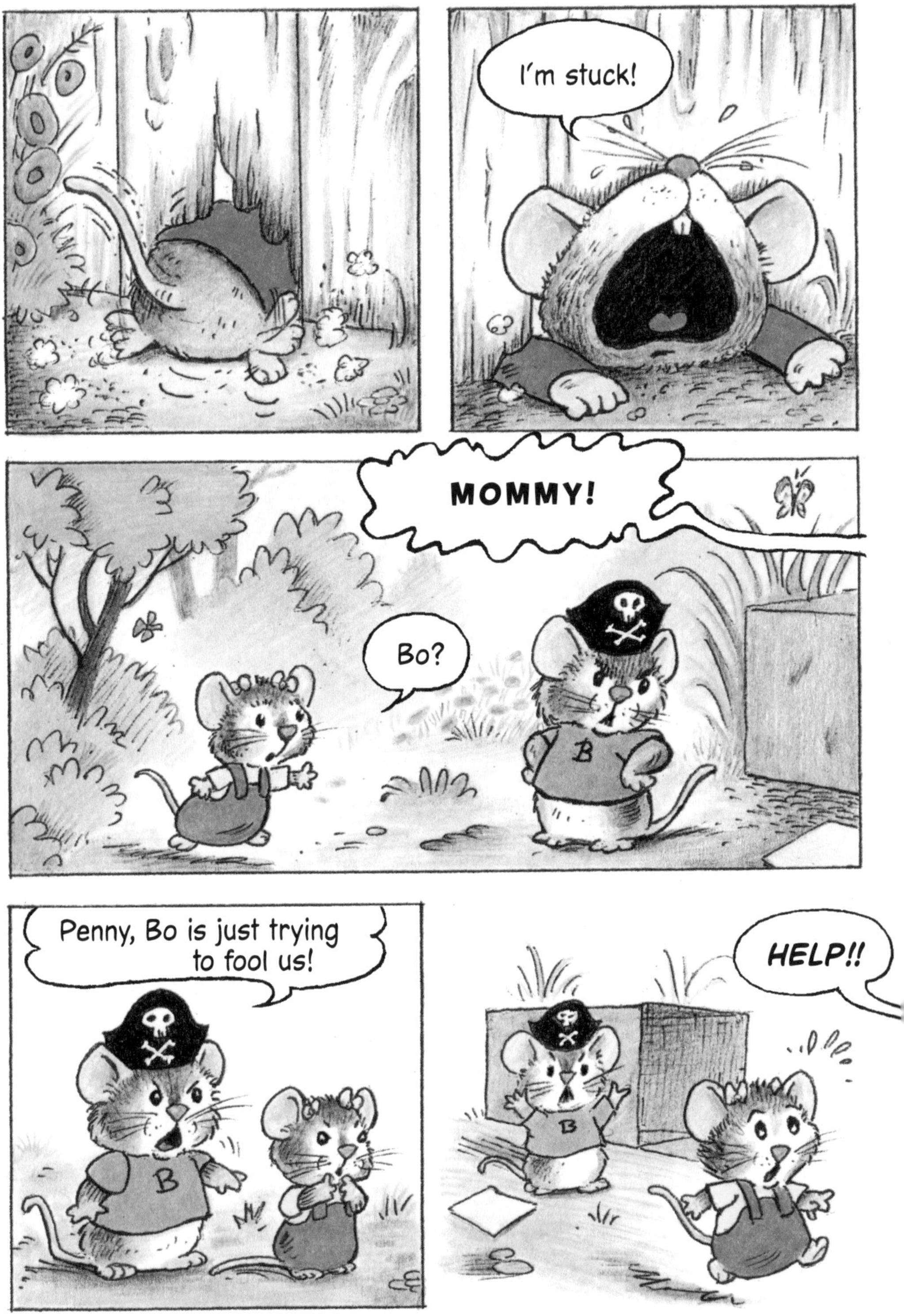
I'm stuck!
MOMMY!
Bo?
Penny, Bo is just trying to fool us!
HELP!!

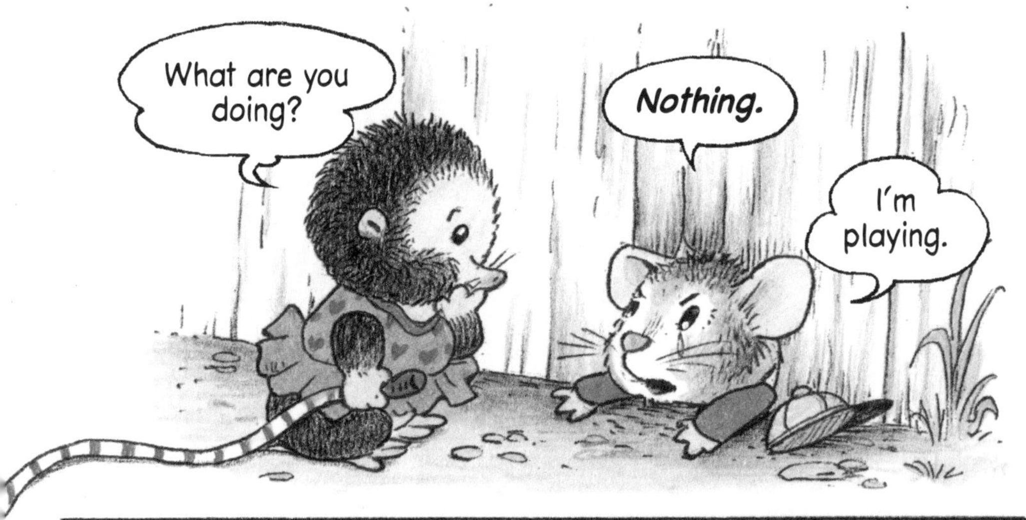
What are you doing?
Nothing.
I'm playing.

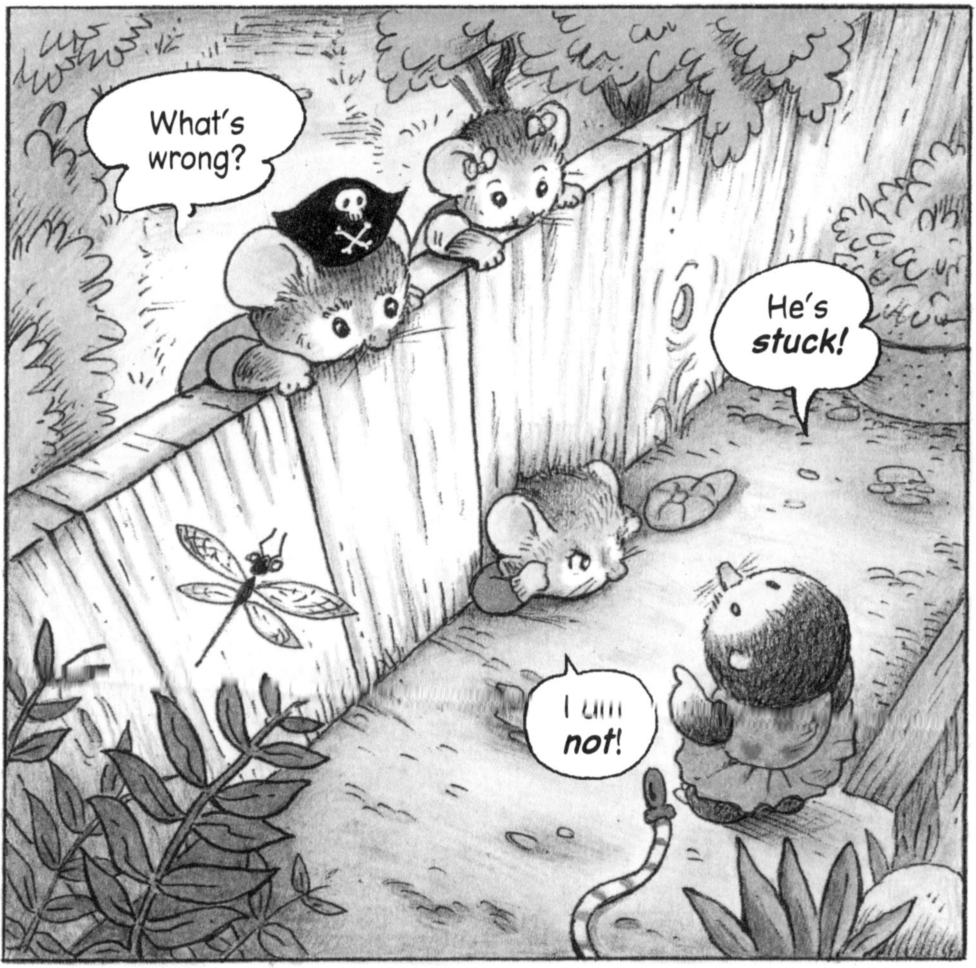
What's wrong?
He's *stuck!*
not!

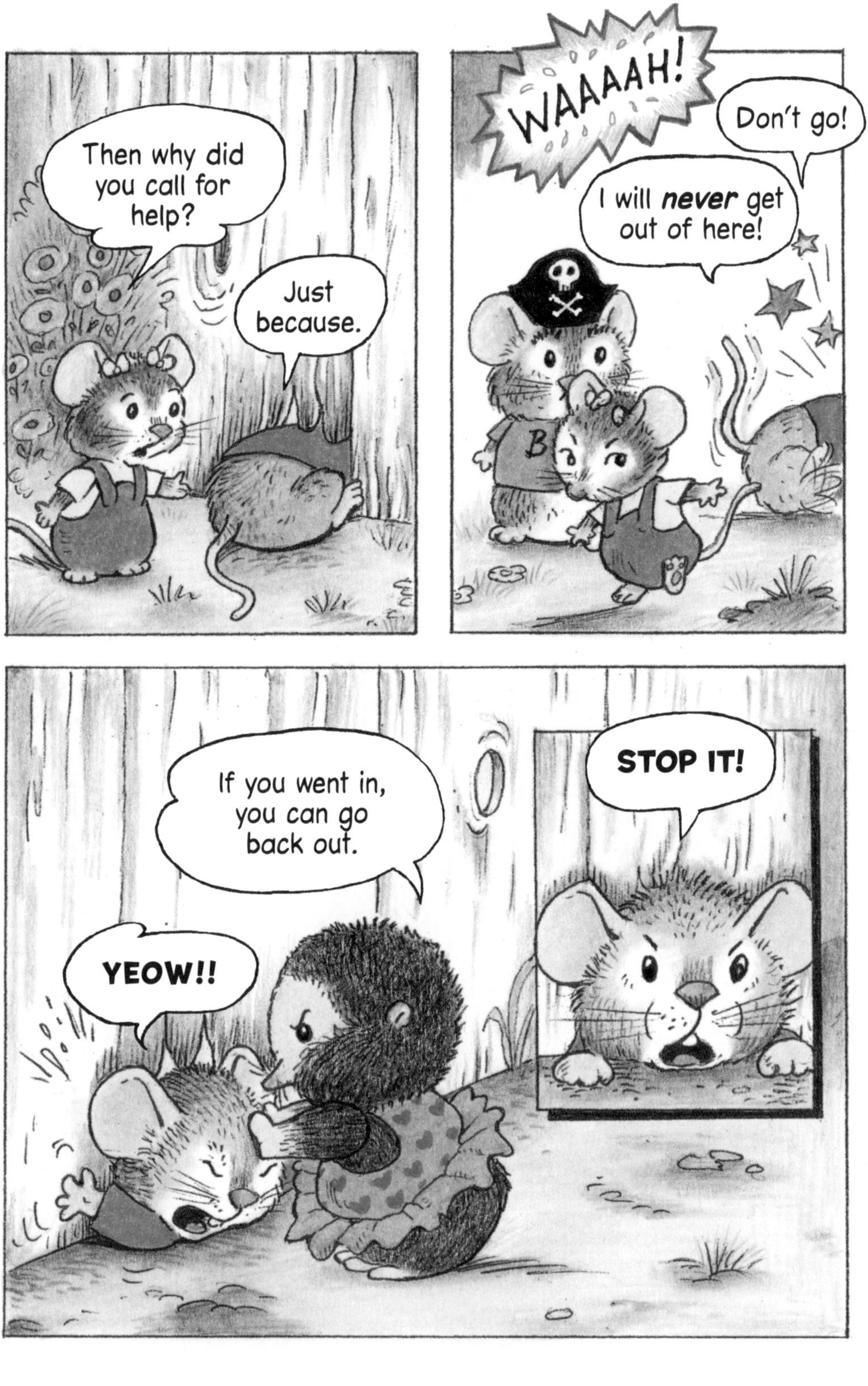
Then why did you call for help?
Just because.
WAAAAH!
I will ***never*** get out of here!
Don't go!
If you went in, you can go back out.
YEOW!!
STOP IT!

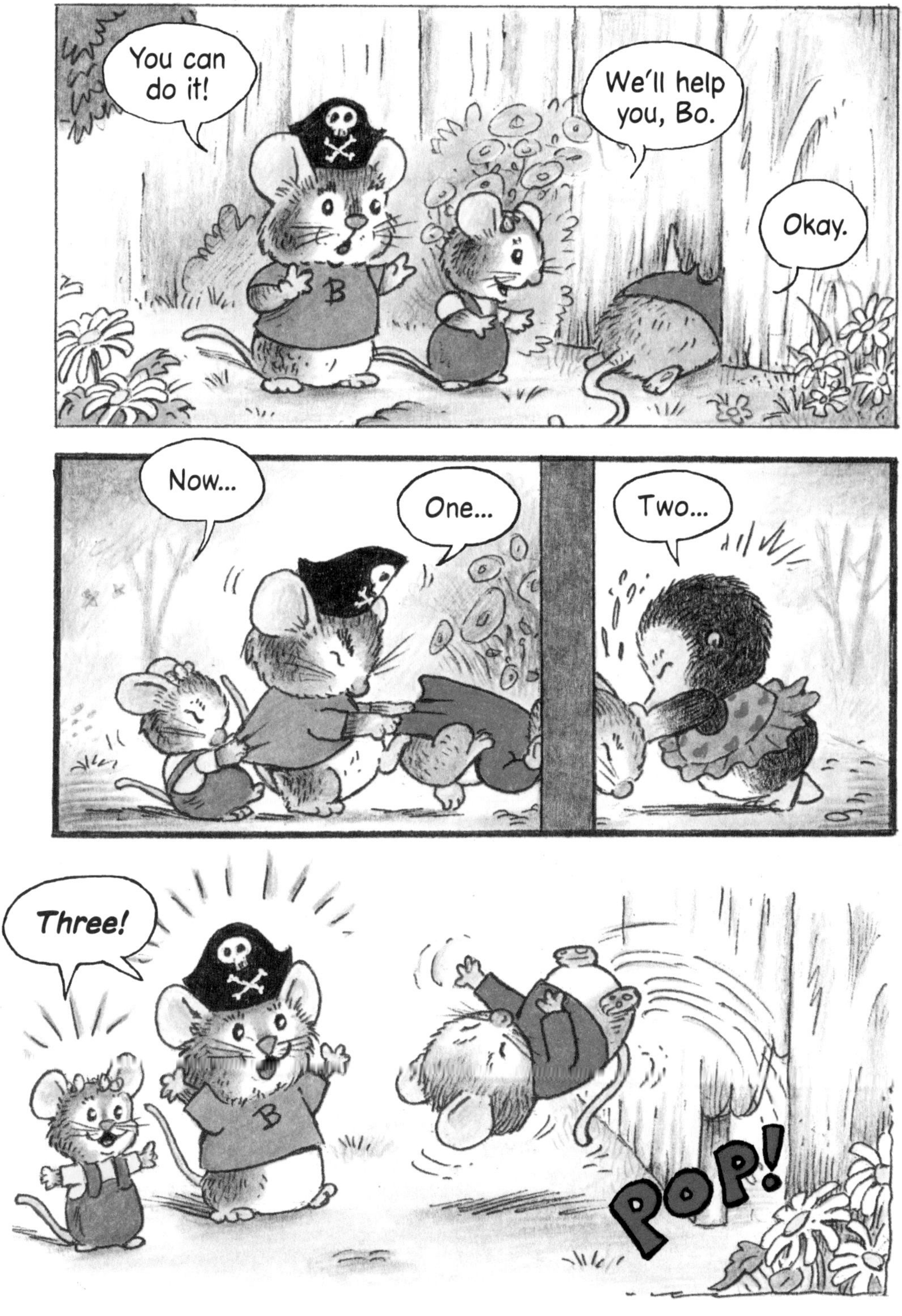
You can do it!
We'll help you, Bo.
Okay.
Now...
One...
Two...
Three!
POP!

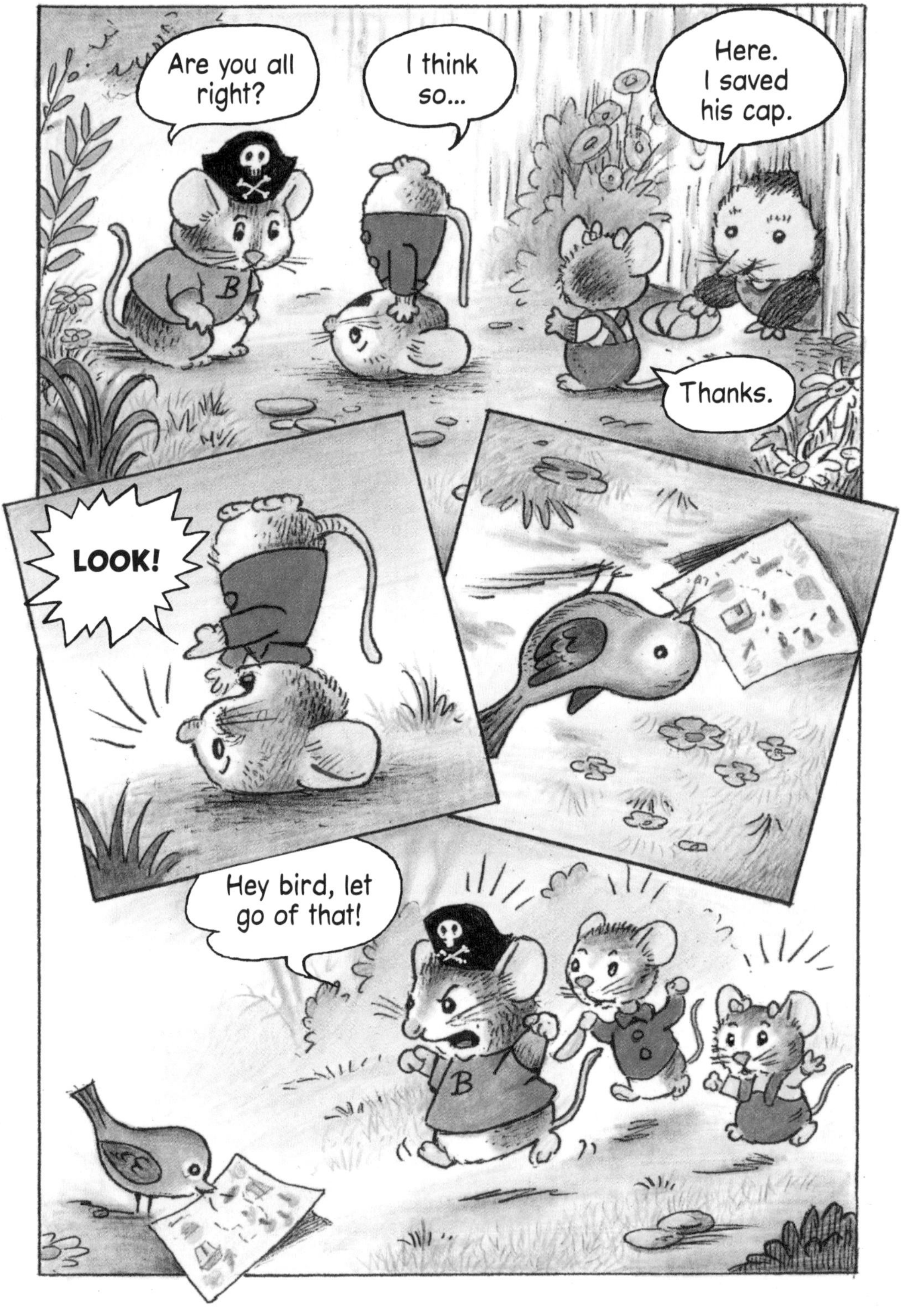
Are you all right?
I think so...
Here. I saved his cap.
Thanks.
LOOK!
Hey bird, let go of that!

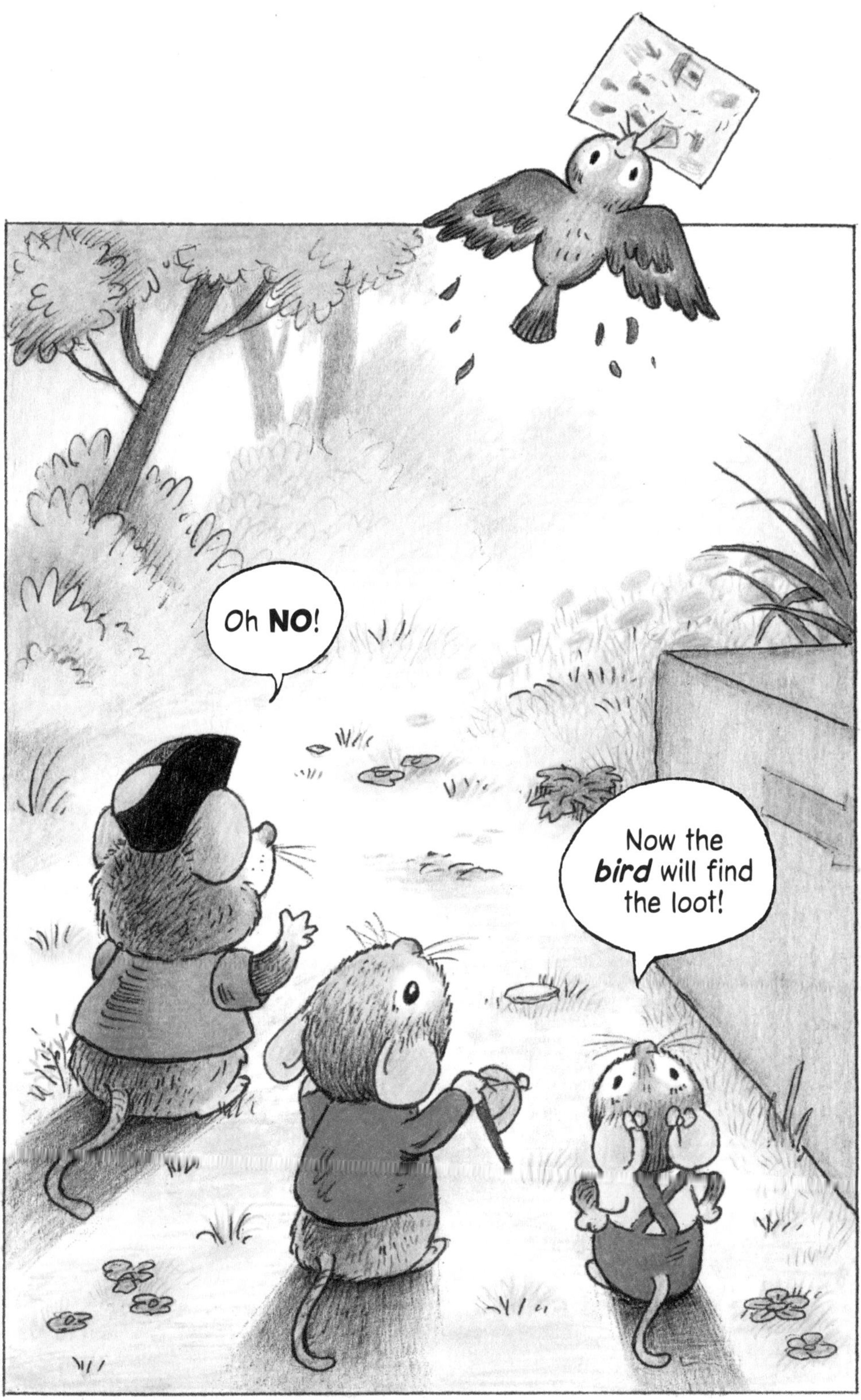
Oh **NO**!
Now the ***bird*** will find the loot!

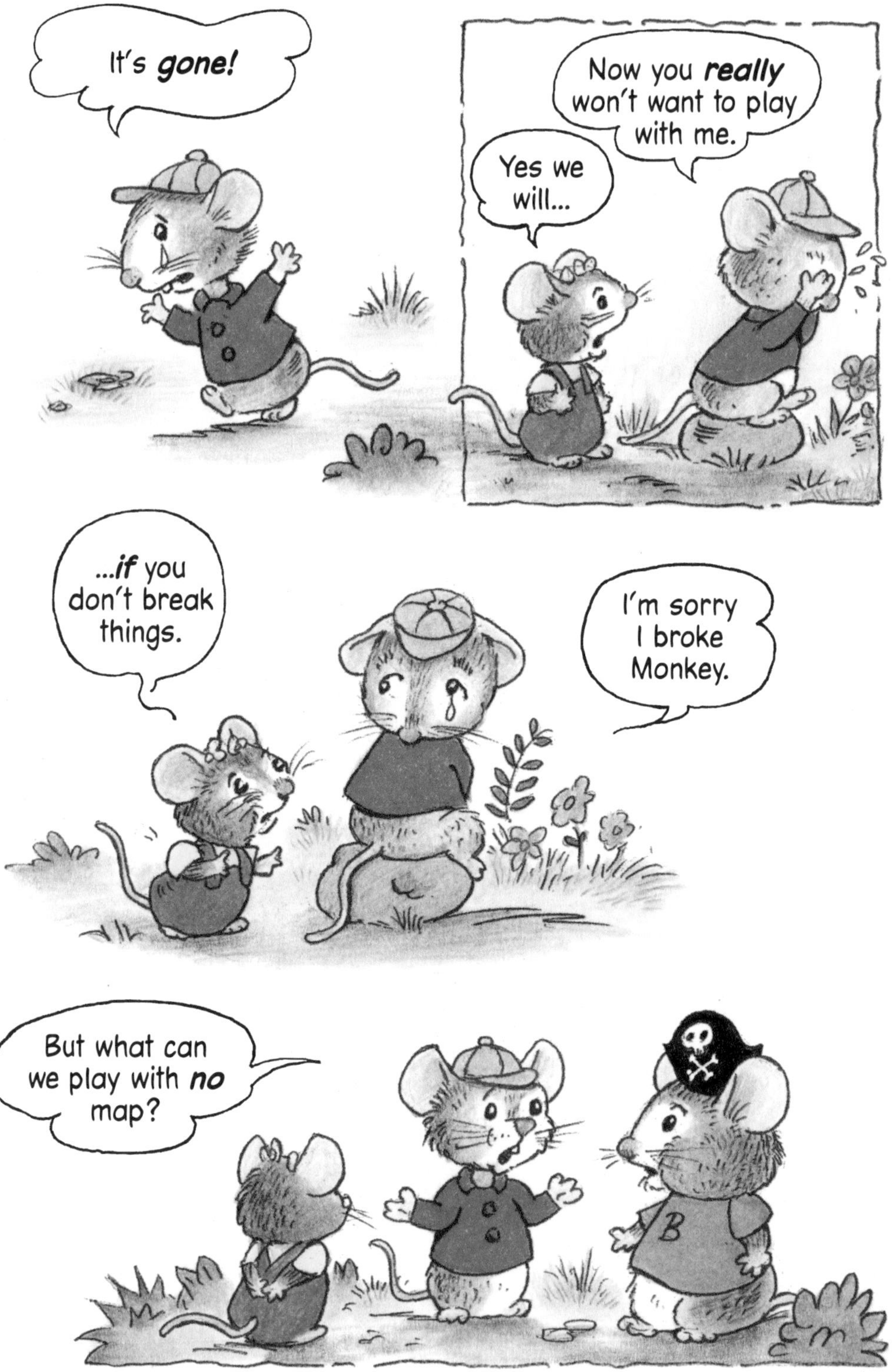
It's *gone!*
Now you *really* won't want to play with me.
Yes we will...
...if you don't break things.
I'm sorry I broke Monkey.
But what can we play with *no* map?

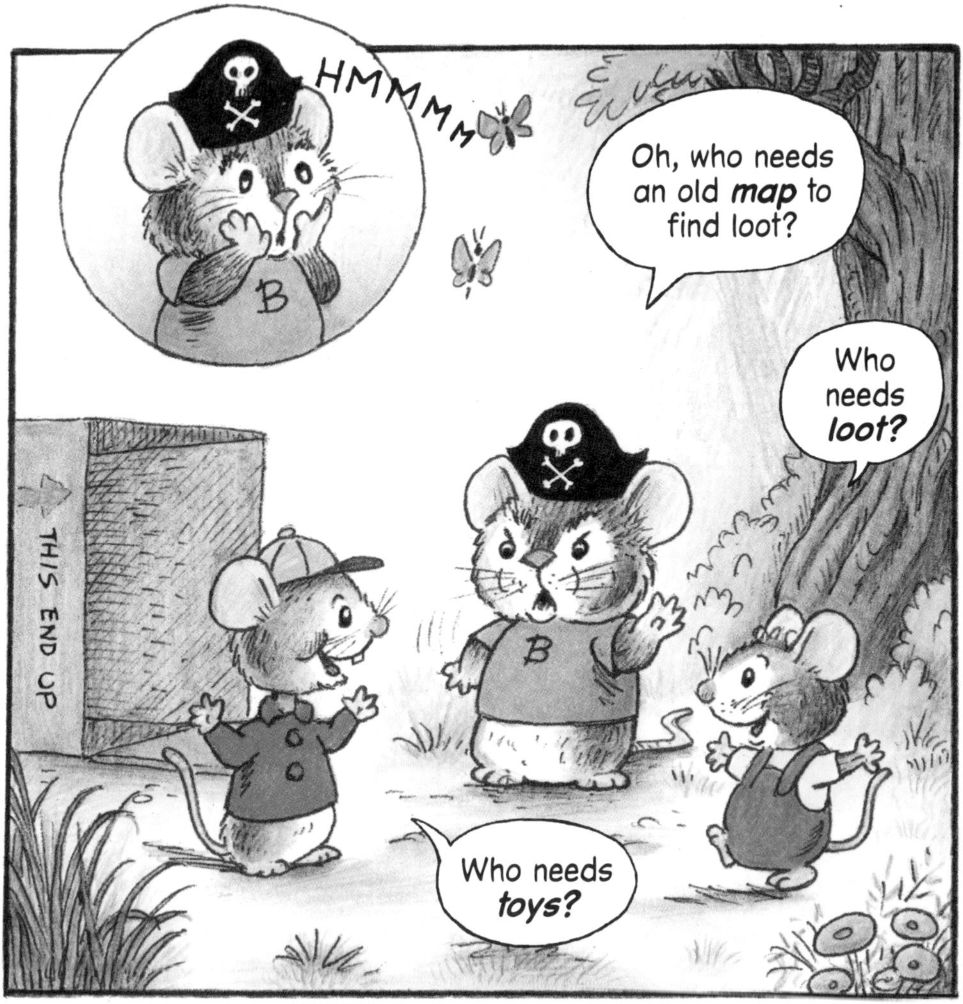
HMMMMM
Oh, who needs an old *map* to find loot?
Who needs *loot?*
THIS END UP
Who needs *toys?*

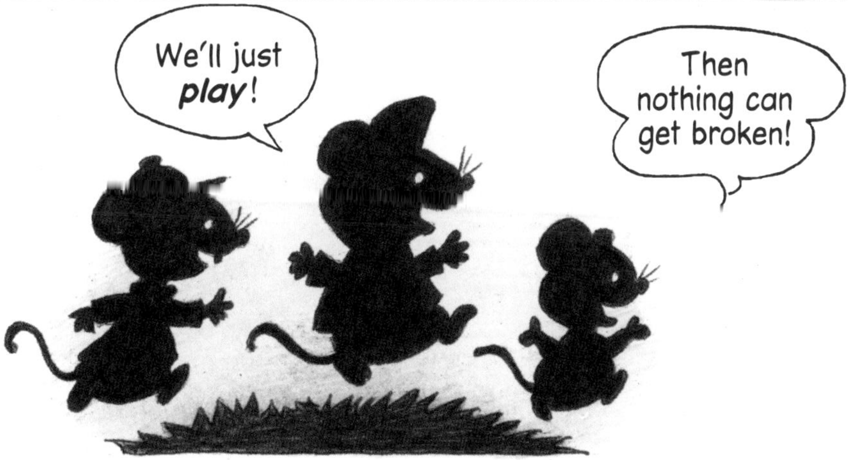
We'll just *play*!
Then nothing can get broken!

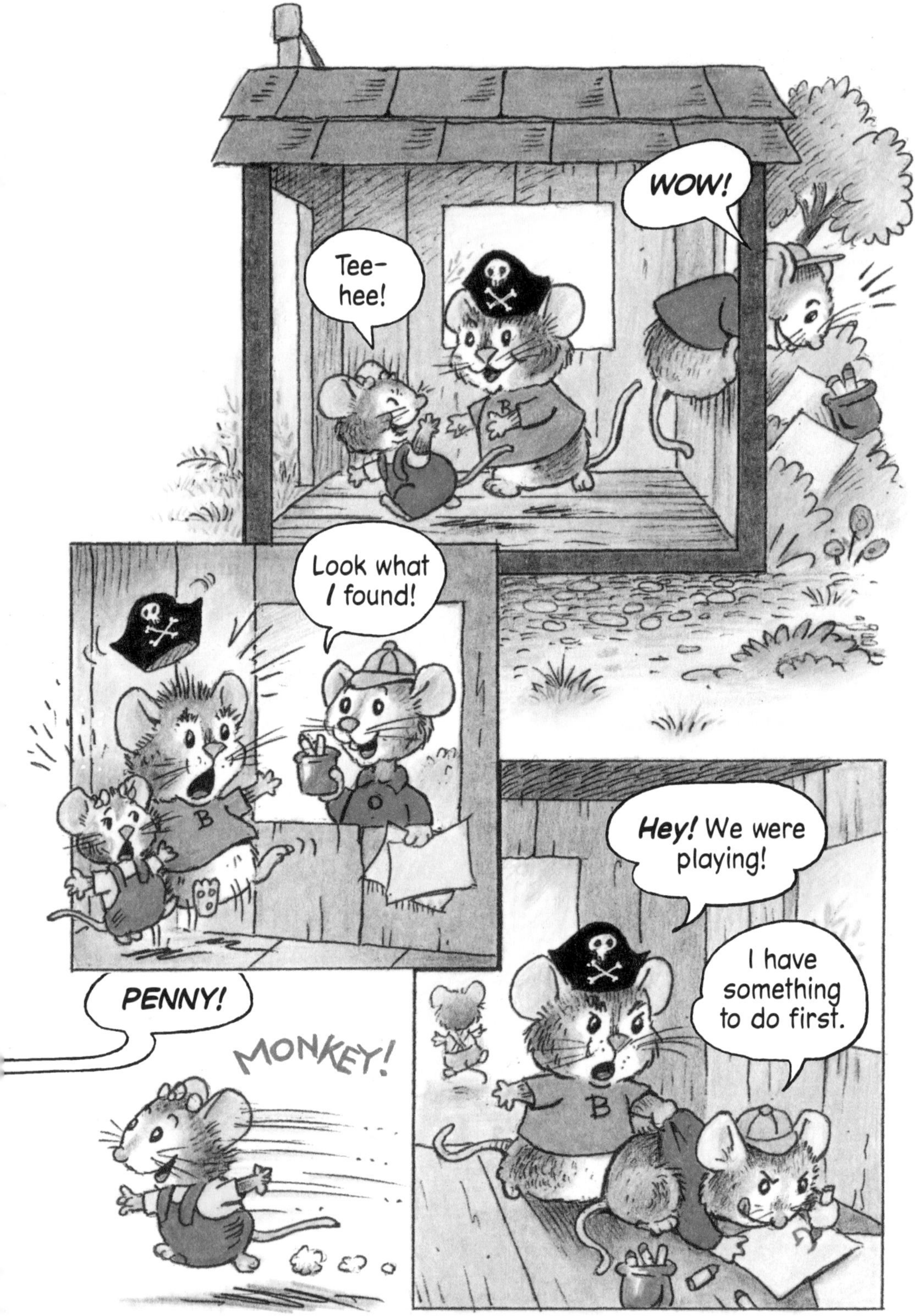
Tee-
hee!
WOW!
Look what
I found!
Hey! We were
playing!
I have
something
to do first.
PENNY!
MONKEY!

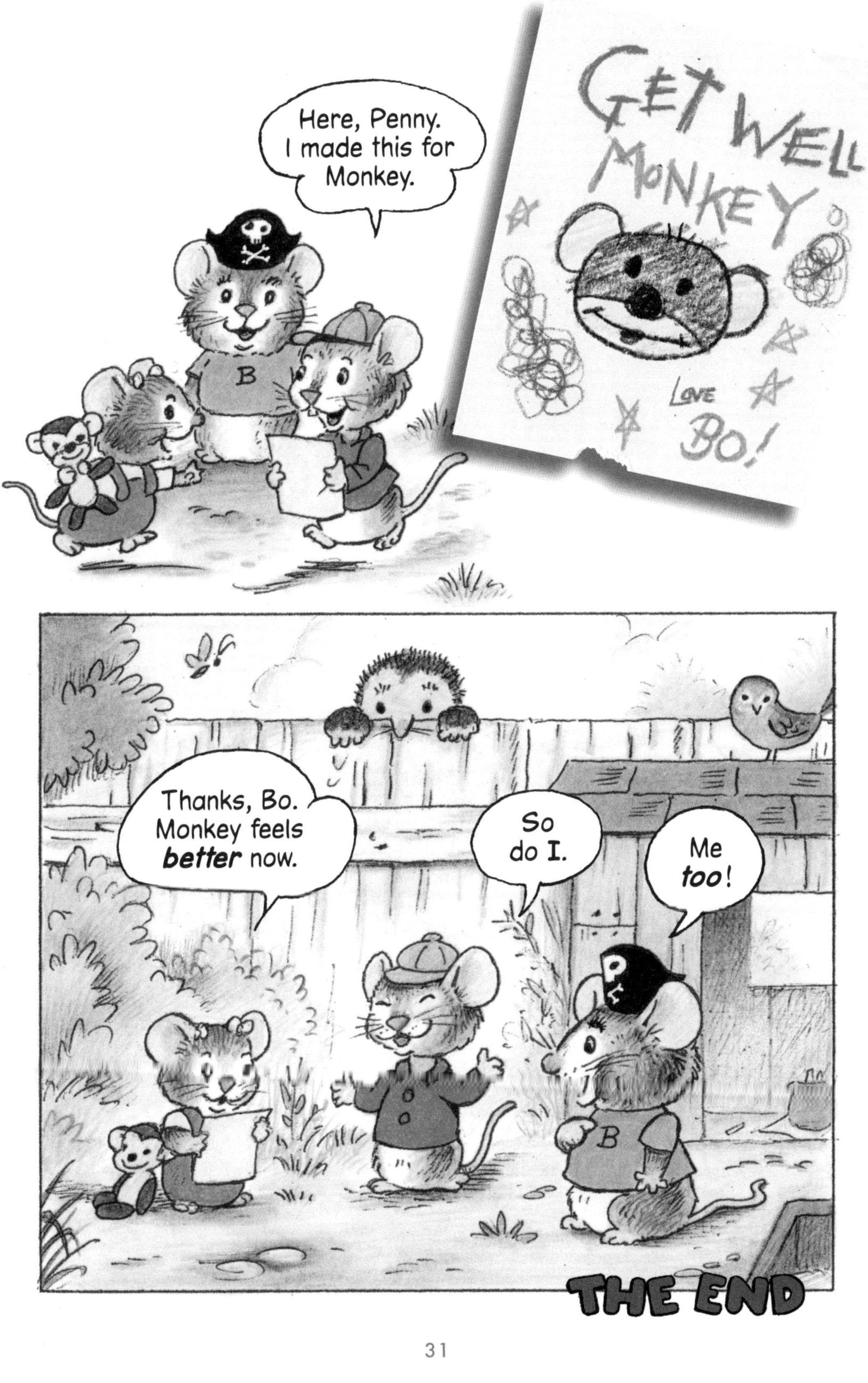
Here, Penny. I made this for Monkey.
GET WELL MONKEY
LOVE BO!
Thanks, Bo. Monkey feels **better** now.
So do **I**.
Me ***too***!
THE END

ABOUT THE AUTHOR

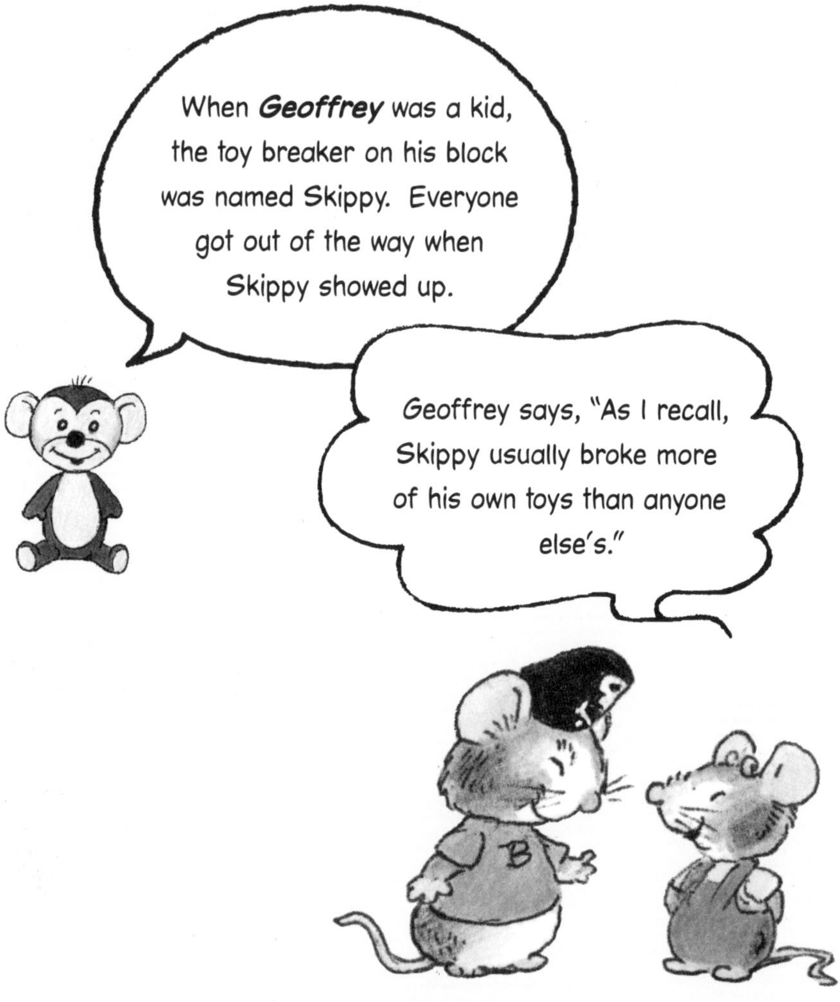
When *Geoffrey* was a kid, the toy breaker on his block was named Skippy. Everyone got out of the way when Skippy showed up.
Geoffrey says, "As I recall, Skippy usually broke more of his own toys than anyone else's."
B

Geoffrey Hayes is the author/illustrator of the Patrick Brown books and of the extremely successful series of early readers Otto and Uncle Tooth. His best-selling TOON Books series, Benny and Penny, has garnered multiple awards. *Benny and Penny in The Big No-No!* won the 2010 Theodor Seuss Geisel Award, given to "the most distinguished American book for beginning readers published during the preceding year." He lives and works in New York City.